I wait.

I wish I could see my watch. How long have I been hiding? It feels like hours. I'm sure it hasn't been, but it feels like it. What if I didn't really hear anything? What if it was just my imagination, or maybe it *was* a cat. Should I just crawl out and move real quietly back to the cottage?

Snap . . . crack . . . snap.

Someone's walking this way and they're not even trying to be quiet anymore.

Also by Greg Logsted

Something Happened

ALIBI
JUNIOR
HIGH

GREG LOGSTED

Aladdin
New York London Toronto Sydney

ALADDIN

An imprint of Simon & Schuster Children's Publishing Division
1230 Avenue of the Americas, New York, NY 10020
First Aladdin paperback edition August 2011
Copyright © 2009 by Greg Logsted
All rights reserved, including the right of reproduction in whole or in part in any form.
ALADDIN is a trademark of Simon & Schuster, Inc., and related logo is a registered trademark of Simon & Schuster, Inc.
Also available in an Aladdin hardcover edition.
For information about special discounts for bulk purchases, please contact Simon & Schuster Special Sales at 1-866-506-1949 or business@simonandschuster.com.
The Simon & Schuster Speakers Bureau can bring authors to your live event.
For more information or to book an event contact the Simon & Schuster Speakers Bureau at 1-866-248-3049 or visit our website at www.simonspeakers.com.
The text of this book was set in Adobe Garamond.
Manufactured in the United States of America 0711 OFF
2 4 6 8 10 9 7 5 3 1
The Library of Congress has cataloged the hardcover edition as follows:
Logsted, Greg.
Alibi Junior High / by Greg Logsted. — 1st Aladdin ed.
p. cm.
Summary: After thirteen-year-old Cody and his father, an undercover agent, are nearly killed, Cody moves in with his aunt in Connecticut, where he is helped with his adjustment to the trials of attending public school for the first time and investigating a threat in nearby woods by a wounded Iraq War veteran.
ISBN 978-1-4169-7959-3 (hc)
[1. Interpersonal relations—Fiction. 2. Junior high schools—Fiction. 3. Schools—Fiction. 4. Aunts—Fiction. 5. Veterans—Fiction. 6. Spies—Fiction. 7. Connecticut—Fiction.] I. Title.
PZ7.L8286Ali 2009
[Fic]—dc22
2008043889
ISBN 978-1-4169-4814-8 (pbk)
ISBN 978-1-4169-9508-1 (eBook)

To Lauren and Jackie,
because once is not enough

Acknowledgments

I'd like to offer a huge thank-you to my editor, Liesa Abrams, for all of her help and support. She's the best. And to my agent, Pamela Harty, for keeping her hands firmly on the wheel. I hate that kind of driving. Special thanks to Andrea Schicke Hirsch, Robert Mayette, and Lauren Catherine for all their patience and advice. You guys rock! Thank you, Jackie Logsted, for being my little girl. Daddy loves you. Words cannot express the gratitude I have for my wife, Lauren Baratz-Logsted. She's an original. I don't know what I would do without her help, guidance, and inspiration. There's nobody I'd rather have by my side.

ALIBI
JUNIOR
HIGH

ARRIVAL

I hate airports. I've been in airports all over the world, but they're basically all the same. Places of painful partings and awkward greetings.

The door opens and I follow the others off the plane, through the skywalk and into the terminal. I scan the room, sizing up the security, looking for emergency exits, and watching for possible hostiles. Nothing seems out of the ordinary but I make a few mental notes. There are eight people worth watching carefully, five to keep an eye on, and I remind myself that the best always blend in so I don't dismiss anyone.

I'm tired. I've been traveling for a week, slicing up my time like an apple. Bouncing from one country to another, one city to another. Switching between planes, trains, boats, and buses.

Living on soda and candy bars. Changing clothes and IDs while trying my best to fit in, to not be noticeable, to never do anything that would make people remember me.

I've been following my dad's prescribed route to Connecticut—a route he guarantees will make me disappear. I'm falling off the map, trying my best to become the invisible boy.

I pass through baggage pickup without stopping. Everything requires that I move quickly; my dad and I agreed that a small carry-on and a garment bag was all I really needed.

I slow down and wait until I see a family passing through security together. I blend in with them. The guard seems sleepy; I doubt he'll remember me.

There are people all around me greeting passengers. Everyone's hugging and crying, taking pictures, shaking hands and slapping backs. The noise level keeps getting higher. It's one huge, emotional paper shredder.

I look around the room and start to worry again. My dad said he trusts her more than anybody, but what if she doesn't show up? What if something's happened to her? What if I don't recognize her? It's been a while since I last saw her, and people can change.

There's a woman by the door. She seems about right: late thirties, medium height, attractive, shoulder-length brown hair, obviously looking for someone. She's also wearing a New York Yankees cap so there's a part of me that actually hopes it's *not* her. Then I get a clear look at her face and the memories come flooding back.

I walk up to her. "Aunt Jenny?"

"Cody?"

"Yes."

She smiles and throws her arms around me. She seems very excited to see me. I'm not sure if I should hug her back so I just keep my arms at my sides. After a while she stops hugging me and places her hands on my shoulders, studying my face.

"Oh, it's so good to see you again. Wow, you look so different. I'm glad you saw me first. It would have taken me a while to recognize you. I haven't seen you in about four years."

"Three years and seven months."

"Um, right. Well." She gives me another big smile. "Welcome to Connecticut!"

"Thanks."

"Do you have any bags?"

I hold them up.

She looks surprised. "That's it? That's all you have?"

"Yes."

She does a little raise of her eyebrow along with a slight shrug. "Well, okay, I guess we can just pick you up some stuff. Your dad certainly sent me more than enough money. You don't need a collection of Rolex watches, do you?"

"No."

"That was a joke."

"Okay."

She looks at me and lets out a short sigh. She seems uncomfortable. "Well, yes, okay. I guess we should get going, right? Do you need anything before we hit the road? Something to eat? Bathroom?"

I look at her cap and remember that day at the café.

"I hate the Yankees."

Her head snaps back. "Okay . . . it's really just a cap; I'm not a fan or anything. I just wear it to keep my hair out of my face when I drive. Do you want me to . . . get rid of it?"

I know I should say no but I keep thinking about the waitress in Santiago, the blood, the smoke, the cap still stuck on her lifeless head. If I have to watch Aunt Jenny walking around every day with that cap on, I think I'll go insane.

Something inside of me feels like it's melting, dissolving, collecting on the floor, and spreading out around me. I let out the word before I have time to pull it back in.

"Yes."

She just stares at me. Maybe I shouldn't have said anything about the cap. Then she starts to laugh, a strange and different sort of laugh. Not like when you laugh during a movie, more like when you lock your keys in the car while it's running and the music is jacked up to the max.

"Fine." She tosses the cap into a nearby garbage can. "What do you say we hit the road?"

I follow her, walking slowly, scanning everything ar[...]
It's great to finally be outside but I find the vastness of the pa[...]
lot disturbing. There's so much space for people to hide in, there's
so much activity.

After walking together in silence for a while it starts to feel
very suffocating. I really should try to communicate. That's what
people do in these situations, right? I clear my throat and say the
first thing I can think of.

"Aunt Jenny Williams, I want to thank you for meeting me at
the airport."

She looks at me for a while. I'm beginning to think I said
something wrong. She smiles, but it's a sad smile. "You're welcome, and just call me Jenny, or you can call me Aunt Jenny if
you want, okay?"

"Okay. I just found out you were my real aunt last week."

She stops walking and looks at me. "Really? Your dad never
told you that I was your mother's sister before?"

"No."

Her eyebrows seem to be trying to reach all the way up to her
hairline. "Never? Even when I came to visit?"

"No—he wants me to call all his girlfriends Aunt This or Aunt
That. I just thought you were one of his girlfriends."

We start to walk again but I feel a shifting in her mood. She's
shaking her head; something has crept under her smiling face.

She raises her chin. "Well, here's my car, Cody."

It's a red Jeep Wrangler. A questionable choice for transportation, as it lacks speed, mobility, and protection, although it's a capable off-road and poor-weather vehicle. The color, of course, is totally wrong. We might as well just drive around all day sending up flares.

She opens the door for me. I toss my bags in the back and buckle myself into the front passenger seat. The radio starts when she turns over the engine; it's set to a pop music station. My dad only listens to opera. His favorite is definitely *The Barber of Seville* but I'm not sure, I think I prefer *Carmen*.

We pay the parking fee and after a few short turns we're heading south on the interstate. The faster we drive the louder she turns up the music. I don't know why but the noise reminds me of the café. Is that how it's going to be from now on? Why can't the past stay where it belongs?

I feel like we're getting boxed in. We're surrounded by cars and trucks. They're too close—they could do anything to us. It's making me nervous. I can feel the sweat starting to flow down my forehead; my heart's pounding, it's getting hard to breathe. I turn to Jenny and attempt to talk over the music. My voice comes out sounding desperate, pleading, like I'm drowning, calling out for help.

"Are you naked?"

She jumps and gives me a puzzled, slightly horrified look. "Am I what?"

"Naked. You know, are you carrying?"

"Carrying?"

"Do you have a weapon?"

Her eyes open wide for a moment and then she actually starts to laugh. "Cody, I don't have a gun. I don't believe in them."

My voice rises even higher. "What do you mean, you *don't believe in guns*? That's like saying you don't believe in knives and forks."

I can see her knuckles growing whiter as she tightens her grip on the steering wheel. She snaps, "Calm down. Statistics show that if you have a gun in your house it's much more likely that it will be used against you or a member of your family."

I moan and slouch lower into my seat. I'm doomed. What was my dad thinking, sending me here? Last week I didn't even know I had an Aunt Jenny. Now I'm supposed to live with her and trust her with my life? I can feel everything slipping away from me.

"You do know what's happened to me, don't you? You know they're after me, right? Shouldn't you have a gun?"

Jenny looks at me. Her hair is whipping around her face. I guess she really did need the cap for driving. She turns down the music. Her voice softens. "Cody, I work with computers and numbers, not guns, but your dad trusts me. Now you're just going to have to trust me, too." She takes one hand off the steering wheel, tucks her hair behind her ears. "I'm sorry. I know you've had a rough time. I know you're scared, but your dad and I are sure you'll be safe here. I wouldn't have agreed to this if I didn't think you'd be safe. Remember, he works for the CIA. If anyone knows how to hide people, it's him. And besides, they're looking for him, not you."

I ease back into my seat. That's exactly what I've been telling myself for the last few days. He wouldn't send me here if he didn't think I'd be completely safe. But I still don't understand why I couldn't have helped him. We've always been a team, we've always watched each other's backs. It's what we do.

"You look tired. You can take a nap if you want. We still have another forty-five minutes before we're home."

I tell her I'm fine and that I don't need a nap, but even as the words leave my mouth I can feel my eyes closing shut. I fight it for a while, but then the radio starts fading into that soft mist of sleep.

It's the same dream I've been having for two weeks. We're back in Santiago; it's the morning that changed my world.

My dad and I are both in a great mood, and we're having break-fast at this small café we've been going to a lot. I like it more than my dad does. The food's just okay but I love sitting outside under the large awning and watching everyone walk by. The friendly wait-resses are beautiful and there's always someone playing guitar in the corner.

We're sitting at a table outside going over some work together, comparing notes, maps, and trying to piece together the schedule of our prospect. We've been following him for a couple weeks, and between the two of us we have his whole routine just about nailed down. We've even found openings for two possible appointments next week.

We're part of what my dad calls "the advance team." We're sent ahead of the main team to put together a file on someone the CIA finds to be dangerous. My dad says our team is so secret, very few people even know we exist.

I've grown to like this kind of paperwork. It's a welcome relief from the constant karate, weapons drills, and homeschooling he puts me through every day.

My dad slaps me on the back and suggests we take a break for the rest of the day, maybe head out to Valle Nevado for some skiing if I think I can keep up with him.

The waitress stops by our table to refill my dad's coffee. She's wearing a New York Yankees cap, which seems very odd to me—a Yankees cap so far from home. She gives me a smile and a quick wink. It's shaping up to be a great day.

I turn to my dad, intending to ask him if he wants to rent skis in town or at the mountain, but I stop. Something's wrong. He's staring at this small blue car that just pulled up in front of the café.

I can see why my father's looking at the car; there's something just not right about the way the driver's acting. He's moving too quickly, too unevenly—he seems very nervous. He glances our way, notices we're looking at him, and then reaches under the front seat. At first

I think he's going for a gun but when he comes up empty-handed I relax a little.

He bolts from the car and races across the street; for a large man he moves quickly, but there's something odd about the way he runs. A car slams on its brakes and nearly hits him; he slides across its hood, lands on his feet, and continues to run. I'm watching but it's just not making sense to me. It's just not sinking in, it's like watching a foreign film with the subtitles in a different language, too.

My dad pulls me to my feet and yells, "Go! Go! Go!" He pushes me through the front door into the restaurant. I plow into a waitress; her plates shower down all around us. I just keep running, my dad's right behind me, pushing me to go faster, yelling for me to head for the back door.

I hear two pops, that's it, just, pop . . . pop.

My dad shouts, "Get down!" and throws me to the floor, covering me with his body. My face is pressed hard against the cold tile.

The blast is the loudest thing I've ever heard in my life. A flash and a burst of light and heat, followed by an unbelievable roar. I hear glass breaking, people screaming, and objects crashing all around us. I feel like I'm tumbling and twisting into a dark, murky tunnel.

I'm not sure how long I float in this distant land of shapeless darkness. When I open my eyes it's raining. I smell smoke and burnt flesh, like a forgotten barbeque. I can't hear anything except this high-pitched ringing. I don't know where I am or why I'm lying on my back in the rain.

It slowly comes back to me; all the pieces sluggishly start sliding themselves together. I call out for my dad but can't hear anything over the ringing in my ears.

I realize the rain is a sprinkler system.

There's someone lying next to me. I look over and see the waitress who had winked at me. Her lifeless eyes are now permanently opened wide and there's a large piece of metal sticking out of the center of her chest. The Yankees cap is still on her head, but it's now soaked in blood and almost unrecognizable.

There's an arm near me, just an arm, and it has a wedding band on the ring finger. I pick my head up and look around at what's left of the restaurant. There's blood and bodies all around me. I start to scream but it's a silent scream. All I can hear is the ringing.

This isn't happening again. This is a dream. Wake up. Wake yourself up!

RECOGNITION

Jenny looks over at me. "Bad dream?"

I try to shake the images out of my head. "Yeah, real bad."

"I'm sorry, but look, we're almost home. See? Here's my street."

We pull onto a street lined with a mix of houses small and large, and tons of American flags. There's a large flag at least every twenty feet. I guess I don't have to worry about forgetting what country I'm living in.

Jenny slows down the Jeep in front of a large yellow house. There's a huge banner outside with bold black letters that reads WELCOME HOME. There must be about thirty people outside, waiting.

We pull into the driveway and I look over at Jenny. She must be able to read my eyes.

"Oh no, Cody. I'm sorry, no. This isn't for you. We live in the cottage out back. Oh, I really should have warned you. I just forgot. My neighbor's son Andy is getting back from Iraq today. Well, actually the hospital, but today's his first day home."

I feel incredibly stupid for thinking that all this might be for me. I look away from Jenny. I'm sure my face must be red. Why would all these people be waiting to see me, anyway? I want to say something clever to keep from feeling so foolish but nothing comes to me.

We stop at the end of the driveway, and we're right in the middle of the group. I don't like being boxed in by people but I tell myself to relax. It feels like a Fourth of July party, someone's even cooking hot dogs and hamburgers. My stomach growls; I guess I'm hungrier than I thought. I get out of the Jeep and Jenny joins me. She waves to a woman in a bright red dress. "So, Beth, today's the big day, huh?"

The large woman hurries over to the Jeep.

"Oh, you know it, Jen! I'm so nervous and excited; it's been so long, he wouldn't let me visit him at the hospital. I can't believe my boy's finally coming home."

"That's fantastic. Oh, and by the way—" She places a hand on my shoulder. "—this is my nephew Cody, the one I've been talking about all week. Cody, this is Mrs. Wheeler."

She sends a big smile my way. "Well, Cody, it's so nice to finally meet you. I've heard so much about you. I'm sure you're going to love our little town. I have a son your age, Albert, he's around here somewhere."

She scans the crowd and spots him. "Albie! Come over here for a second. There's someone I want you to meet."

I look over by the garage and see this really small blond-haired guy. He might be my age but he looks like he could be three years younger. He's wearing baggy jeans and a faded New York Mets T-shirt, and he's talking into a cell phone.

He looks over, suddenly very excited, then he starts jumping up and down and shouting, "Ma! He's coming! He's coming! He just pulled into the street!"

Mrs. Wheeler puts out her hand and steadies herself against the roof of the Jeep. I thought she'd be jumping up and down like Albert but she looks like she's about to faint. "Oh, I can't believe it. I just can't believe it, my baby's finally coming home. My baby."

Music starts blasting from speakers propped up in one of the windows. It's an old dance-type song that I've heard before, it goes, *"Celebrate good times, come on!"*

Someone at the end of the driveway yells, "I can see him! I see him! Here he comes!"

Everyone starts cheering; a few people grab WELCOME HOME! signs that I hadn't seen and start dancing around with them. Some kids light sparklers; they flicker like large birthday candles.

A black Suburban with tinted windows pulls into the driveway and slowly inches toward us before parking by the garage; a couple of guys start drumming on the side of the car. The cheering grows louder.

A chant of "Andy, Andy, Andy!" starts, and soon everyone's chanting along. I don't even know the guy but I feel a surge of excitement.

The passenger door opens and a tall guy eases out of the car. His broad shoulders strain his uniform and he's squinting against the bright sunlight. His left arm is missing and the sleeve of his jacket is pinned up to his shoulder.

Mrs. Wheeler starts crying and runs to him. The crowd parts, and Andy turns and holds out his one arm. His mother falls against his chest and wraps her large arms around him. She sobs, "Oh, my sweet baby! My baby's home, my beautiful baby's finally home."

I look over at Jenny. She's wiping a tear away from her eye.

Andy yells over his mother's shoulder, "Where's my Albie? Albie, where are you?"

I look over by the corner of the garage and I see the little guy still standing there. He seems scared. The crowd starts pushing him toward his older brother. Andy yells, "Hey, little hero! What are you doing over there?"

Albert finally makes up his mind and runs to his brother, throwing his arms around him. "Andy, you're home! You're really, really home. I don't believe it."

"Believe it, buddy. I promised you I'd be back, and I don't break my promises."

"Don't go away again. Don't you ever go away again. Will you promise me that?"

"Yeah, little hero. I promise. No more wars for me."

"I missed you so much. I prayed every night that you'd come home."

"I missed you too."

Albert shifts from one foot to the other. "Sorry about your arm."

"Well, guess what—so am I. But you know what? They tell me they're going to give me a new one. The best money can buy."

Andy starts to work the crowd, shaking hands and joking with old friends. Jenny pats me on the shoulder.

"Why don't I show you the cottage and get you settled in? I'll introduce you to Andy when things calm down a bit."

I grab my bags and follow her across the driveway. The music's still blasting and everyone's having a great time. I glance over at Andy and we make eye contact. He gives me a little nod; I'm about to nod back when I hear gunfire, three quick *pop*s.

I drop to the driveway; the asphalt digs into the palms of my hands. I hear more and more *pop*s. I look toward the sound and realize it's just a couple of kids setting off a pack of firecrackers. I push myself off the driveway, embarrassed and humiliated. People are looking at me. Jenny reaches down to help me up.

Andy's being helped off the ground, too. His mother and Albert are pulling him to his feet. We make eye contact again, only this time it's not a hello.

It's recognition.

SHADOWS AND STARS

I hate sleep. It lies to me, it makes its promise, and then where does it go? It leaves me here, twisting all alone in the darkness.

I'm out of my bed again, out of my bed before I go out of my mind. If I have to be restless I'd rather it be under the stars than under my sheets. I slip out the side door and into the shadows, a new raccoon with a kitchen knife for claws, roaming the night.

I move slowly and silently, like walking through sand on the beach. At first I keep close to the cottage, always trying to blend in with the surroundings, always listening for anything unusual. Later I move farther outward in a large loop through the woods.

I can't shake this feeling that I'm being watched. It's what's been keeping me up at night. I lie in bed and sense there's someone out in the darkness studying me, searching for a weakness, looking for an opening just like my father and I have done so many times before.

It's been like this for the whole week. Every night I can't sleep until I walk my loop. When I'm satisfied there's nobody watching me I slip back into the cottage and finally fall asleep. Jenny can't understand why I always look so tired in the mornings.

I had hoped that tonight would be different and I'd be able to fall right to sleep. Tomorrow's going to be my first day of school. I've been trying to delay it for as long as possible, building this little sand castle of independence, but Jenny insists and I know she's right.

We've had a good week together; it almost felt like a vacation. She's been great, helping me settle in, picking out clothes, and letting me set up my room so it feels like mine. This is the first time I've ever had a room of my own. It's nice, really nice. I'm not sure what I'm going to put up on the walls but I'll figure it out soon.

I'm surprised how comfortable I feel with Aunt Jenny. We sit together at night and read. Sometimes I'll look over the top of my book and study her face, her expressions, the movements of her hands and I'll wonder, How much of my mother does she share? I have no memories of my mother. Her face might as well have been a watercolor left out in the rain, washed off to white.

I've completed the loop through the woods and I'm about to head through the tall hedges by the street. It's easy to slip through them; it gives me a great view of the main house, driveway, street, and the front of our cottage out back.

Snap.

What's that? I stand perfectly still; I even hold my breath. I know I heard something. I inch my back up against a tree. I try to blend in with it, to become part of it.

Time stretches on. I can hear the trees creaking gently in the breeze and an owl hooting from someplace deep in the woods. I hear a distant train blowing its whistle; it's a lonely, sad sound that makes me shudder.

Maybe it was nothing, a falling pinecone or something like that. Still, I wait, and when I think I've waited long enough, I wait some more.

Crackle.

I'm positive I heard something that time and it's close, maybe twenty feet to my right. I squat down and slide the kitchen knife out of my back pocket. My heart is pounding and I'm struggling to control my breathing.

Snap.

It's getting closer. Maybe it's an animal, a cat, a dog, or even something wild. Always expect the worst; always be prepared.

I look around me. Dad told me if you don't have what you want, work with what you have. I can't find anything useful as an added weapon, but I notice a thick, low bush. I lie on my stomach and silently slither under it; the branches scratch my back but allow me just enough room to fully conceal myself.

The dirt is damp and smells like worms. I have a handful of wet leaves down the front of my shirt. They scratch and itch but I don't dare try to remove them; it might make noise. I'm alert but I've begun to relax a little. If someone's looking for me they'll only find me if I move.

I wait.

I wish I could see my watch. How long have I been hiding? It feels like hours. I'm sure it hasn't been, but it feels like it. What if I didn't really hear anything? What if it was just my imagination, or maybe it *was* a cat. Should I just crawl out and move real quietly back to the cottage?

Snap . . . crack . . . snap.

Someone's walking this way and they're not even trying to be quiet anymore. They're getting closer. I peer out from under the bush. My heart starts to pound again and I struggle to control my breathing.

I see a pair of black boots approaching. They look like they're just going to walk past, but they stop by the tree that I'd been leaning against. A man squats down and checks the ground. I think he's found something, maybe a footprint.

He looks my way; I grip my knife tighter. I can't make out who it is until he moves slightly and the moonlight falls across his face. He looks real familiar. Then I notice the missing arm.

It's Andy.

He stands up and starts to walk away, but stops. His voice cuts through the silence. Even though it's at a volume that wouldn't be out of place in a library, it sounds like a shout.

"Cody, I'm impressed. I'm not sure if you're here or gone or, come to think about it, if you were ever here at all, but if you can hear me, we should talk."

I watch his dark form slowly walk back to the main house, open a side door a few inches, and slide inside.

PANCAKES AND BAD PENNIES

"Cody, didn't you set your alarm?"

"Huh?"

Jenny switches to a singsong voice. "Co . . . dee! Wake . . . uuuup!"

"Letmesleep."

"You're going to be late. Come on, it's your first day of school."

"I'llstarttomorrow."

She sits on my bed and the mattress sinks from the weight of her body. "Come on. It's time to get ready."

I slowly open my eyes. They feel like they've been pasted shut. I blink them a few times before I manage to keep them open but it's a struggle. Jenny's looking at me, smiling, and then her expression changes, suddenly alarmed.

"Cody, you're a mess! You're all scratched up and covered in dirt! What's going on?"

It all comes rushing back to me: hiding under the bush, sneaking into the cottage, doing my best to quietly clean up in the bathroom without turning on the lights or running the water. Being so tired I could hardly keep my eyes open. My plan was to wake up before Jenny and take a shower.

What a way to start the day. I don't think I'll be able to talk myself out of this one. Sleepwalking? Nah, that wouldn't fly. I guess I should try to dance as close to the truth as possible.

"I couldn't sleep, so I went out for a walk."

"You went out for a *walk*?"

"Yes."

She looks skeptical. "It's obvious you went out. What I want to know is why. And don't tell me it's because you couldn't sleep."

I might as well tell her. "I kept getting this feeling that someone was watching us. I had to make sure no one was out there."

"So you just marched out there? That sounds like a great plan. What if someone *was* watching us?"

"I was careful. Nobody can see me if I don't want them to."

"Cody, that was stupid. No more. If anything happens to you your dad will kill me. From now on you don't leave this house at night without my permission. You hear me?"

"I hear you."

"I still don't understand how you got covered in dirt."

I lean forward. "Turns out there *was* someone out there. I had to hide under a bush."

Jenny glances toward the window. "You mean someone's watching us?"

"I'm not sure. No, I don't think so. I don't know."

"Cody, I'm confused." She runs her hands through her hair. "Was there or wasn't there someone outside last night?"

"There was."

"Well, who was it?"

"Andy."

"Our neighbor? He's watching us?"

"No, I don't think he's watching us. I think we both just happened to be outside. It was weird." I think about the way he moved quietly around me. "He's really good, too."

Jenny stands up and walks to my window. "Cody, the guy's an *Army Ranger*, he's spent the last six years in Special Ops, of course he's good." She shakes her head. "Sneaking around in the middle of the night like that—you're lucky you didn't get yourself killed. What were you thinking? No more. You hear me? *No more.*"

"Okay, I hear you."

"I hope so. Now, get yourself ready for school. You're running late."

I take a shower and get dressed.

I join Jenny in the kitchen. She's making pancakes. I forgot how good pancakes smell. I can't remember the last time I've had them. I think it was about a year ago at that little place in Switzerland.

She gives me an approving nod. "Well, you're looking better."

"Thanks."

"Hungry? Want some pancakes?"

"Definitely."

She brings two tall stacks to the kitchen table and we attack them. I guess we were both hungry. Jenny keeps shoveling pancakes into her mouth but it doesn't stop her from talking. "So, you nervous?"

"About Andy or my dad?"

"About school. After all, you've never been to a real school before. I know your dad's done a fantastic job teaching you, but this is going to be different."

I shake my head and almost laugh. "School? Why should I be nervous about school? Thanks to Dad my English and math skills are on a college level. I speak five different languages. I have two black belts. I've been to every corner of the globe and I've been in more dangerous situations in any given month than most of those kids have been in their whole lives."

I give her a dismissive wave. "Trust me. Going to school with a bunch of small-town kids is not something I'm worrying about right now."

Am I standing at the right corner? Jenny said the bus stops at the end of the street. This is the end of the street, right? I check my watch again. I'm not early; I'm right on time. Shouldn't there be other kids here by now? What if I missed the bus? What if it came early?

Wait, here comes somebody.

It's a girl—cute, with long black hair and strange clothes. She's loudly chattering away on her cell phone. It's like listening to a truck full of broken dishes driving down a dirt road.

She stops and stands about ten feet away from me and continues ranting into her phone, complaining about some guy she met and how he used to talk to her but now he doesn't and she thinks this girl named Penny, who she calls 'Bad Penny,' had something to do with it because apparently she's responsible for everything that goes wrong with this girl's life, and she hates her, she really does, she just hates her.

We make eye contact and I blurt out, "Hi." But she doesn't say anything to me, she just continues talking into her phone. It makes me feel incredibly stupid for saying anything to her and annoyed that she couldn't have at least said hi back to me.

She glances my way again.

"I take back the 'hi.'"

"Excuse me?"

"I take back the 'hi.'"

"What's your problem?"

"Normally when someone says 'Hi,' the proper response in return is 'Hi.' I said 'Hi,' you didn't say 'Hi' in return, so I'm taking my 'Hi' back."

"Okay, you want a 'Hi'? . . . *Hi.* . . . Are you happy now? What a twisted psycho. Just leave me alone . . . loser."

She cups her hand over her phone, walks farther away, and starts talking about me in a hushed voice. Each word that I overhear somehow makes me feel like I'm evaporating bit by bit.

Another girl, with short red hair, joins us at the bus stop. She has her iPod ear buds firmly in place and I can hear the faint sound of music pumping into her head. She bobs slightly from side to side and stares straight ahead. I don't bother saying hello.

"Hey, Cody."

I turn around and see Albert walking toward me. "Hi, Albert."

He stands next to me. "First day, huh?"

"Yes."

"Nervous?"

"No."

The bus turns the corner and starts bouncing toward us. Albert looks at me strangely.

"What are you wearing?"

"What do you mean?"

"You're wearing that to school?"

I look at my clothes. "What's wrong with them?"

"Everything. The shorts are way too short, your socks way

too long, and nobody tucks in their T-shirt. You're dressed like somebody's dad."

"Really? Somebody's dad? Um, how about the backpack?"

He gives it a quick look then just shakes his head.

The bus stops next to me, its doors swing open. The driver is a large woman wearing an old Yankees cap. Perfect. Almost every seat is occupied; the bus is loud and buzzing with energy. I slowly walk up the rubber-coated steps, and for the first time it sinks in that I'm really entering a new and foreign land.

A land I know nothing about.

SMALL SLIVER OF SEAT

I've been on lots of buses all over the world. City buses, country buses, new buses, buses so old you're sure they're not safe. I've ridden on buses full of rich businessmen and buses full of people so poor you can almost feel their hunger.

One time I rode for hours on a long, winding dirt road through the mountains—one wrong move on the driver's part and we would have tumbled hundreds of feet to our deaths.

All those experiences should have been enough to prepare me for this moment, but right now I feel more uncomfortable than I've ever felt on a bus, any bus, anywhere. I'll take that terrifying ride through the mountains over this anytime.

A school bus lives in its own special time zone, a time zone unlike any other. It's a place where time doesn't exactly stop; it just slowly decays like a dead deer left by the side of the road.

When I first walked up the stairs of the bus everyone stared at me. Except the few people with open seats—they just gazed straight ahead, avoiding eye contact. I could feel them willing me not to sit with them, sending out strong vibes for me to keep moving along.

It looked like there was an open seat at the back of the bus but when I got there the whole seat was missing. I turned around to look for another and realized they were by then all occupied. I just stood there, feeling like the loser in a kids' game of musical chairs.

Normally if a bus is full you get off and wait for the next one. I don't think that's going to work here. School buses seem a lot like quicksand, easy to walk into, not so easy to get out of.

The bus driver barks, "You gotta sit down!"

I can see her in the rearview mirror, staring at me from under her Yankees cap. She's really mad but I'm not sure why. It's not my fault the bus is full.

Everyone turns around and looks at me.

"You have to sit down! I can't drive the bus until you sit down."

Some guy in the front yells, "Don't sit down—I've got a first period history test!"

Everyone starts to laugh. I know they're laughing at the joke but it somehow feels like they're laughing at me. Maybe they are.

"Will you please sit down!"

I look around the bus wondering where she expects me to sit. I shout, "There's no place to sit!"

She turns around, clearly getting more aggravated. "Just triple up! Come on, you're going to make everyone late."

I look at the seat next to me. A guy wearing a leather jacket mutters, "Don't even think about it."

I move down the aisle. Everyone keeps glaring at me. Nobody wants me to squeeze next to them; it's easy to see why.

I'm walking past Cell Phone Girl.

The driver shouts, "Just sit down already!"

I plop down on the edge of her seat. She lets out a heavy sigh, looks up from her phone and mumbles, "Perfect . . . just perfect. I get to sit next to the psycho new kid. Just don't touch me. You hear me?"

She doesn't move over, not even an inch; she just continues with her mindless texts. I sit there with only half my butt on the seat, my legs in the aisle, and my patience stretched to the max. I throw my backpack on the floor. I can't believe I've got to carry that thing around all day.

The bus pulls out into traffic. It's even harder to sit like this once we start moving. I'm struggling to stay in place while trying my best not to touch Cell Phone Girl. I think it would be easier to walk on my hands to school.

"You're going to have to move over."

She looks up. "Are you talking to me?"

"Yes."

"There's no room."

"Yes, there is. Move over."

She rolls her eyes. "Hey, I didn't ask you to sit here."

"True, but *I'm* asking you to move over."

She smirks and raises her eyebrows. "And *I'm* telling *you* there's no room."

My hand darts out and snatches the cell phone from her grip. It takes her a moment to realize what just happened.

I eye the open window and hiss, "Move over or your cell phone's leaving the bus before you."

She moves her arm in an attempt to grab back her phone but I quickly flip the phone from my right to left hand.

"Try that again and it's definitely going out the window." Just to let her know I mean business, I start flipping the phone back and forth between my outstretched hands with blinding speed. The hours I've spent practicing with my nunchucks make this flashy exhibition amazingly simple.

"Gimme back my phone!"

"Move over first."

Cell Phone Girl looks over at the small, dark-haired girl sitting next to her.

"Do you believe this psycho?"

The girl doesn't say a word; she seems hypnotized by the flying cell phone. There's a slight smile tugging at her lips and her eyes are opened wide.

Cell Phone Girl huffs, "Move over so I can get my phone back."

The small girl scoots over as close as she can get to the window, Cell Phone Girl moves over with her. This finally allows me enough room to get my whole butt on the seat.

I give her a sideways glance and sarcastically say, "That wasn't so hard now, was it?"

"Gimme back my phone."

I place it in her hand and she grabs it like a fumbled football, pulling it close to her body. She stares straight ahead and sinks into an angry frozen silence. I guess she's decided I'm not one to be messed with.

Two guys next to me are arguing about some video game—I guess there's a right way and a wrong way of doing level fifteen. I don't have a clue what they're talking about.

A hat sails by me.

Someone shouts, "Hey! What did you do that for?"

The bus driver barks, "Knock it off back there!"

Two girls are laughing hysterically behind me. It doesn't seem possible that anything could be that funny. One of them keeps saying, "Did he really say that?"

I realize that Cell Phone Girl's leg is gently pressing up against mine—the whole leg, from the hip to her ankle. Was it always like that? I don't think so. Is she trying to intimidate me? Trying to get me to move away from her? Move myself back to the edge of my seat? Well, if she is, it's not going to work.

I t worked.

By the time we get to the school, my leg muscles are cramping up from holding on to my small sliver of seat and my right butt cheek is so numb it might as well have been pumped full of Novocain. I smell like perfume from when Cell Phone Girl 'accidentally' spilled some on me. She's called me names that I've never heard before and hope I don't ever have to hear again.

I'm the first to stand up when the bus stops at the sidewalk, the first down the aisle, and the first out the door.

BEND AND BLEND

The morning sun blazes off the mirrored front doors, blinding everyone who approaches the school. Walking toward the building is like walking straight into a ten-thousand-watt lightbulb. I'm beginning to feel like a moth.

I study my shadow, stretching from my feet and reaching for the school. It always seems so confident, this silent dark knight of mine. If something gets in its way it will just bend and blend over it. I envy my shadow.

The door swings open just as I'm about to reach for it, and it slams against the wall. Some guy in a brown sweatshirt bolts past me. He's laughing and running from a bigger kid who's trying to shoot at him with a water pistol. A blast of cold water hits me right in the face; it's shocking and I do a weird little twitch.

A group of guys in the corner laugh. They're standing together like a small tribe. One of them imitates me; he twists up his face, blinks his eyes, and jumps backward. They all laugh harder.

Great, I'm in the school for less than a minute and I've managed to get myself shot. I put my head down and set off toward the office.

"Yo!"

Jenny and I were at the school yesterday and they told me I should report to the office first thing in the morning to go over a few things.

"Yo! . . . Yo!"

I'm not really sure why we couldn't have gone over stuff yesterday. I was there, they were there, but hey, why not wait until tomorrow?

"Yo!"

Is somebody 'yo'-ing at me?

I hear running behind me. Judging by the sound of the shoes pounding on the tile floor I'm guessing it's a fairly large man, maybe two hundred and fifty pounds, around thirty years old, most likely a former athlete with a past knee injury. There's something desperate about the way he's running. Those are definitely aggravated footsteps. I sense danger.

I wait until he's within my zone, then I pivot on the ball of my left foot, look over my shoulder, and ready myself for an upward strike with the heel of my right foot. He's a large man so my first kick will be directed at his nose; it's stunning and painful and normally stops even the most aggressive attacker in his tracks.

My mind is focused and my muscles are tensing, readying themselves for battle. I'm about to pull the trigger when I notice the uniform. It's the school security guard. I ease off and stand down. I was one second from laying him out on the floor. My guess is that's something they'd frown upon around here.

"Hey! Didn't you hear me calling you?" He's just as large and aggravated as I thought he'd be, maybe even more so.

I raise my shoulders and hold out my hands, palms facing up. "I didn't know you were calling me."

"Who else would I be calling?"

I look around the crowded hall. "I don't know . . . there's about fifty other possibilities."

"Don't you give me any of your lip."

"I'm just answering your question."

He jabs me in the chest with his finger. "You're giving me lip."

I don't know. Maybe I should have laid him out on the floor when I had the chance. I'm guessing it would have set a school record for the quickest suspension, but right now it feels like it would have been worth it.

"Do you go to this school?"

"Yes."

"How come I've never seen you here before?"

"It's my first day."

He looks skeptical. Then he takes out a small notepad from his top pocket. On the outside flap of his pocket I notice his name tag: S. Boyle. "What's your name?"

"Cody Saron."

He writes down my name, then studies my face like an artist readying himself to paint a portrait. Other kids are stopping to watch us.

"Well, Mr. Cody. Why don't you follow me to the main office."

Great. That's all I need, to be escorted to the office by an over-stuffed goon in a cheap, tight uniform.

I give him my best smile. "That's okay. I know where it is. Anyway . . . aren't you supposed to be watching the door?"

I'm guessing that this was the wrong answer. Two little veins on his temples suddenly throb to life, and his eyes get this incredibly fierce, wild look to them. Clearly, this guy has some kind of an anger-management problem. Maybe he abuses steroids; I've heard that bursts of rage are a common side effect of steroid abuse. I'm thinking that's what the *S* on his name tag must stand for: "Steroid" Boyle.

He starts poking me in the chest again. "Listen, don't you go telling me what my job is. My job is to watch out for the safety and well being of the students. This isn't a mall. You can't just walk in off the street and start wandering around."

I hold up my hands again, palms up. "Who said anything about wandering? I was on my way to the office."

"Not without me."

I give up the fight, which seems to be drawing more attention to me anyhow, and fall in for my escorted trip to the office. Steroid Boyle plods down the crowded hall, parting kids like a snowplow. I walk quietly beside him and find myself thinking about my dad. He wouldn't have let anyone talk to him like that. I've seen him shut bigger guys up with just a look.

My dad likes to talk about "respect." He says there's two ways of getting it: you either earn it, or you take it. I'm not earning or taking anything; I'm being led around like a puppy.

Everyone is staring at me, whispering, wondering, and most likely creating vicious stories. All I wanted to do was to slip in quietly and quickly blend in. Instead, here I am, part of an odd two-person parade, consisting of a chest-thumping gorilla and his reluctant sidekick, the boy who envies his own shadow.

Our journey finally ends at the office. Two women are busy with paperwork behind desks. A tall counter separates us from their workspace.

Steroid Boyle clears his throat to get the younger woman's attention. "Good morning, Jane."

She looks up from her work, clearly tired, bored, and not in the mood. "Hey, Steve. What's up?"

So the *S* stands for Steve, not Steroid. I guess I'll just have to think of him as Steroid Steve from now on.

"Caught this guy sneaking into the school."

My head snaps up. I try to keep the anger out of my voice but it's difficult. "I wasn't *sneaking* in. I just *walked* in the front door. How's that sneaking?"

He leans over the counter. "Guy's got a real *attitude* problem, too."

My voice rises, coming close to a shout. "*Attitude problem? What are you talking about? You're the one with the attitude!*"

A woman's stern voice calls out from behind me, "Mr. Saron!"

I recognize the voice from yesterday. It's Mrs. Owens, the school's assistant principal, a humorless, middle-aged woman who wears dark suits, crisp white blouses, and styles her brown hair in an amazingly tight bun.

Slowly, reluctantly, I turn myself around and greet the cold woman with as much warmth as I can muster. "Hello, Mrs. Owens."

I give her a smile but she doesn't return it. I have doubts that she ever really smiles.

"Why don't you step into my office?"

Steroid Steve gives me a little nod and smirks. I really should have kicked him in the nose.

I follow Mrs. Owens into her dark little office with its drawn blinds and shelves full of dusty old books. She sits behind her large polished desk. I'm about to sit in one of the brown leather chairs opposite it but she glares at me.

"Will you please shut the door."

"Oh, sorry."

I close the thick wooden door, notice an old Yankees pennant hanging on the inside, and return to the leather chair; the cushion makes a hissing sound when I sit down.

Mrs. Owens has some papers spread out on her desk and we sit together in silence as she reads them. The minutes stretch on. I look around the room. There are no photographs of her family on the walls or on her desk, just diplomas and books. When my dad and I used to case our prospects he would say an office like this indicates a complete lack of any real social life. I glance at her left hand: no wedding band.

I wonder if I'm expected to talk first. It's kind of odd that we're just sitting here like this. I watch her reading for a while, debating if I should say something.

Finally I say, "Mrs. Owens?"

She looks up at me; the expression on her face might as well be a huge question mark.

"Um, you wanted to see me?"

She gives me a dismissive wave of her hand and returns to her papers. What's that supposed to mean?

I watch as she continues to read. More time passes. I'm not getting all this. Why am I here if she doesn't want to talk to me?

Finally she looks up. "Well, Mr. Saron, how are you?"

"Um, fine, Mrs. Owens."

"I've been reading over your transcripts."

My transcripts, right. I forgot all about them. Why didn't she tell me that's what she was reading? My dad created this whole new background for me; it's somewhat privileged but basically normal.

"Mr. Saron, I'm impressed. You've attended private schools in Argentina, France, Japan, and for the last three years, England. Not only that, you have excelled academically in each of these different scholastic environments. Very nice."

I mumble, "Thank you," and avoid eye contact. Even though my dad and I went over all of this for a few hours our last night together, the less I talk about it now the better. You never know when some small little detail will trip you up.

"However, there are a few things I'm concerned about."

I look up. What is she talking about?

"Many of your past schools have noted that you require a great deal of discipline, that you can be unruly and have trouble with authority figures. Is that true?"

What? Where did that come from? What is she talking about? We didn't put anything like that in the transcripts.

"Tell me, is it true, Mr. Saron?"

"Um, no, it's not true."

She leans forward and looks me in the eye. "Why do you suppose so many of your teachers would mention a discipline problem if it wasn't true?"

That's a good question. Did she make that stuff up or did my dad put it in my records? Why would my dad do that? Then I remember how he's always stressing the importance of hard work and discipline. Yeah, that's it. He put it there to make sure everyone pushes me hard and keeps me honest. That's my dad.

"Excuse me, Mr. Saron, did I say something you find amusing?"

"What do you mean?"

"That smirk on your face. I suggest you wipe it off."

I didn't realize I was smirking.

"Sorry, Mrs. Owens, but really, I wasn't smirking."

"It sure looked like you were to me. Let's get a few things straight here. Number one, we have a zero-tolerance policy for violence. You fight and you're automatically suspended. Understand?"

"Yes, ma'am."

"Absolutely no weapons of any kind are to ever enter our school. Violation of that rule will get you kicked out of school permanently. Understood?"

"Yes, ma'am."

No weapons? That's just great. What happens if someone comes after me at school? Is Steroid Steve going to protect me?

"We have a code of conduct on the first page of our student handbook. You're expected to read it, know it, and follow it. Understood?"

"Yes, ma'am."

Mrs. Owens just stares at me for a while. I feel like s... me up, arriving at some kind of a conclusion.

"I certainly hope that you and I are going to get along. I like to run a tight ship. I do not want any trouble from you, young man. Do you understand?"

"Yes, ma'am."

She rises to her feet. "Oh, one more thing. I've been wondering—you've always attended private schools. Why the switch to a public school now?"

I remember the blue car, running through the café, the huge explosion, the smell of smoke and burnt flesh, the dead and the dying, the severed arm, the waitress's lifeless eyes.

"Um, well . . . my dad's got some problems with his business, so we had to make some changes."

She walks around her desk and mumbles "Sorry to hear that," before extending her hand and giving me what I can only assume is a smile. "Let me be the first to say, welcome to Northridge Junior High."

Another hour passes before I'm able to get out of the offices. I'm sent to my guidance counselor, Miss DeNitto, an extremely hyper little woman who drinks way too much coffee. She's also one of the most unorganized people I've ever met. The first five minutes of our meeting is spent looking for her glasses.

After we find her glasses, which were next to the coffee maker, she hunts for and finds with slightly less difficulty my class schedule. I'm impressed. Judging by the state of her desk, which is piled high with folders and paper, I had serious doubts that she would ever find it.

We spend at least fifteen minutes in her closet-size office, going over every little detail of my schedule. She shows me the teacher's name, the name of the class, the location of the class, she highlights the number of the classroom. She even brings out a map of the school and highlights a route for me to follow so I don't get lost.

I've just spent a week traveling around the world, following plane, train, and bus schedules, yet I'm being treated like the most difficult journey I'll ever have to undertake in my life is the one between Spanish and history.

Miss DeNitto gives me a huge smile. "Any more questions about your class schedule?"

"Uh, no, I think you've covered just about everything."

I look at the schedule and it hits me that I'll actually have to go to all these classes. Every single day I'll be expected to be someplace at a certain time. I've never had to do anything like that before. I try to imagine what it will be like and the only thing that comes to mind is a sink slowly dripping in the night, driving you insane.

I stand to leave.

"Mr. Saron, we're not quite done here. I'm required to go over the student handbook with you."

I sit back down.

We go over the handbook, page by page, or should I say Miss DeNitto goes over the handbook. I sit by her side and grunt at the appropriate times. It's endless, simplistic, and incredibly boring. That sink has started to drip.

My mind drifts. I wish I were back at the cottage with Aunt Jenny. Yesterday she showed me a bunch of old photographs. The one I really liked was a picture of my mother and Jenny wading in a lake with my dad. It looked like they weren't much older than me. They all had their pant legs pulled up and large smiles stretched across their faces. There was a happiness in my dad's eyes that I'd never seen before.

I asked her if I could keep it. I put it in a little wooden frame. It's on my nightstand next to the alarm clock.

Something catches my eye. A girl walks into the outer office. I can't stop looking at her. She glides across the room; it's like she owns the space that surrounds her. I'm drawn to her smile, her hair, those big brown eyes.

She's beautiful.

One of the secretaries is talking to her. They're laughing. The girl reaches for something and then jumps back, the secretary springs to her feet. There's a large cup of coffee on its side. The brown expanding puddle quickly overtakes papers on the desk. Everyone's frantically running for paper towels.

"Cody?"

"Um, yeah?"

"Are you paying attention?"

I turn away from the coffee cup circus. "What? Oh, yeah, sure. Passes in the hall."

She stands up and closes the handbook. "I guess that's it. Any questions?"

I rise to my feet and motion at the girl running with the paper towels. "I was wondering if you know who that girl is?"

Miss DeNitto looks across the room. "Which one?"

"Um, the one who just knocked over the potted plant."

"Oh, that's Renee Carrington. She helps out around the office. She's a bit of a klutz but she's a really sweet girl. Would you like to meet her?"

I look across the room. The secretary's still mopping up the coffee from her desk. Renee is on her hands and knees scooping potting soil off the floor. The plant that used to occupy the pot looks hopelessly mangled. She has a huge apologetic smile stretched across her face.

I don't think anyone has ever looked better.

"Come on. I'll introduce you."

There's this ball of fear that suddenly grows in my chest and quickly spreads through my body. It's a different type of fear than I'm used to. This kind robs your self-confidence and keeps words from forming on your tongue. I suddenly can't think of anything

I could talk to her about. There's not a doubt in my mind that if I were to meet her right now I'd just stand there like a mindless, wordless zombie.

I put on my most confident smile. "Oh, that's okay. Maybe later. I think I'd like to . . . you know, uh, go to my classes or something."

Fifteen right, twenty-six left, right eight, and . . . nothing! I kick the locker. I can't believe it. I've been trying to open this thing forever. I check the number again. Nope, it's the right locker. I check the card Miss DeNitto gave me. Nope, I'm dialing the right numbers. This combination must be wrong. I give it another kick, this time even harder.

"Young man! Is there a problem here?" I jump and turn around. There's an angry teacher standing a few feet away from me. She has the type of face that's ageless; it's impossible to tell whether she's twenty-five or forty-five.

I mumble, "No problem, just trying to open this locker."

"Speak up. I can't hear you."

A small crowd starts to form around us. I hear a girl say to her friend, "Look at his shorts and socks." They both laugh.

I try to speak louder but it comes out sounding more like a shout. "I'm just trying to open this locker!"

"Kicking it is not the way to open it. Did you try the combination?"

I throw up my arms. "Of course I tried the combination. It doesn't work."

"Did you spin past the second number?"

I try to keep the frustration out of my voice but it bleeds through. "Of course I did. What do I look like, an idiot?"

Mrs. Ageless takes the card out of my hand and quickly spins the numbers. The door clicks open. Everyone laughs like she just pulled an elephant out of a hat.

I raise my hand; at first Mrs. Smith ignores me but then she looks my way. "What is it now, Mr. Saron?"

I rise to my feet. "Actually the First World War wasn't really the first world war. Many scholars consider it to be the eighth. You had the Nine Years' War, the War of Spanish Succession, the War of the Austrian Succession, the Seven Years' War, then you had the War of American Rev—"

"Mr. Saron!"

I look at Mrs. Smith. She seems very annoyed. "Yes?"

"Didn't I tell you before to stop interrupting me?"

"I raised my hand."

She grabs a pen and paper off her desk and starts writing something on it. I can tell she's really angry, although I'm not sure what I did wrong. Then she marches across the room and slaps the paper into my hand.

"I want you to take this to Mrs. Owens's office."

The class starts making *Ooooh* sounds. Mrs. Smith barks, "Quiet! There will be none of that!"

I gather my books and quickly glance around the room. Everyone seems to be happy that I'm getting kicked out of class. I don't understand why. The girl I saw in the office, the beautiful one, Renee Carrington, isn't even looking at me; she's just drawing something in her notebook. I don't think I've impressed her. Figures.

As I walk past her desk she looks up at me and it's as if something explodes inside me. I'm not sure if I should smile, nod, or keep my face expressionless. I can feel my brain firing all these different thoughts at the same time.

Her eyes are so beautiful.

Something suddenly catches my foot and I feel myself stumbling forward. I come close to falling but awkwardly manage to stay on my feet.

Everyone starts to laugh and I quickly turn my eyes to the door and move toward it. All I want in this world right now is to be out of this room.

I look at my plate. "Excuse me, what is this?"

The older woman runs the back of her gloved hand across her forehead and then adjusts her hairnet. She snorts. "It's lunch."

I stare at the red ooze leaking out of a bun. "No, really, what do you call it?"

"It's the Cowboy Burger."

I pick up the tray and examine the burger, trying to figure out what's inside. It doesn't look like anything I've ever seen before. "What's in a Cowboy Burger?"

A tall kid behind me lets out a long, exaggerated sigh and says, "It's like a Sloppy Joe."

"What's a Sloppy Joe?"

He rolls his eyes. "You've never had a Sloppy Joe?"

"Of course not. What's in it?"

"How can you not have ever had a Sloppy Joe? I thought everyone knows what Sloppy Joes are. It's you know, like hamburger, but mushy like chili and not as spicy. Kind of like meat sauce."

I can't believe what I'm hearing. "And whose idea was it to put it on a roll? How do you eat it?"

He picks up his tray and walks around me. "Listen, I don't care if you eat it. I just want to eat *my* lunch."

There are a few things I'm familiar with and I pile them onto my tray. It looks like my lunch will mainly consist of side dishes and desserts.

I'm waiting in line at the register when the comments start again. "Mr. Shorty Shorts" and your basic "Socks" seem to be the most common. I find that just ignoring them seems to work best, but it's hard. I look at my "Sloppy Joe"; there are things I'd love to do with it and none of them involves me putting it into my mouth.

After paying for my lunch, I look around for someplace to sit. It's strange, the way the seating arrangement works out. It's not like anyone is telling me where I can and can't sit, but people have a way of looking at you that keeps you moving along.

In the end I sit by myself in the corner.

I'm hurrying down a hallway. This doesn't make any sense. There are two floors and three blocks, A block, B block, and C block, but they're not in order. It should go A, B, C, right? Not A, C, B. And these numbers! If you're going to number rooms, you should number them in order. Not odd numbers here, even there.

The bell goes off. I'm late again.

I take out the map that Miss DeNitto made for me. I study it and wonder why I can't seem to figure out where I am. Two girls walk past me. I'm about to ask them for help when one of them says, "Hey, it's Mr. Shorty Shorts." They giggle as they walk away.

The hall quickly empties. Doors are closing all around me. I'm alone in a hall that twenty seconds ago was packed with kids. When the last door closes the sound echoes. I stand there feeling even more lost. I'm overwhelmed by a sense of frustrating incompetence. I've never felt anything like this before.

THREADING A NEEDLE
WITH WORDS

I wait for the bus to drive off before swinging my backpack over my shoulder. I look up and notice Jenny waiting for me in her Jeep. It's idling on the side of the road and I can hear faint music. She offers me a quick wave and a welcoming grin.

I open the door and heave my full backpack into the backseat before plopping down beside her.

"Hey, Cody! How was your first day of school?"

I don't say anything. I can't. I'm too angry. I just sit there and stare out the window, listening to one of her mindless pop songs on the radio.

After a while she lets out a huge, almost comical, sigh. "Oh, come on. I'm dying to know. Tell me about your school."

I explode. "You really want to know? It's stupid! That's what it is. I hate that place. It's so stupid!"

She turns off the Jeep, places her hand gently on my shoulder, and turns toward me. "Hey, what's going on? Talk to me."

"I hate that place. It's so stupid!"

"Yes, you said that. Now tell me why."

"Why? Where do I start? Everything about it is stupid." I point at my full backpack in the rear seat, and my voice grows even louder. "Look at that thing. My dad and I hiked over the Andes with smaller packs than that! It's insane!"

"I'm sorry, hon. Do you have a lot of homework?"

"No! That's the stupid part of it. I just have a lot of books! Teachers want me to read two pages from one book and one page from another. Before you know it, I'm hauling around forty pounds of books to read twenty pages. It's so stupid!"

Jenny rubs my shoulder. "Hey, calm down. It's all going to work out. Maybe you could read ahead or something like that."

She twitches her nose and backs away a little. "Um, by the way, are you wearing . . . really strong perfume?"

I throw up my arms. "Still? I've heard that all day! Don't get me started. I do *not* want to talk about Cell Phone Girl!"

"Cell Phone Girl?"

"I said I don't want to talk about Cell Phone Girl!"

She holds up her hands defensively. "Fine, fine. We don't have to talk about anything you don't want to."

I fume. "That girl's just plain evil. I bet the walls turn black when she walks into a room."

"No problem. We don't have to talk about her. We'll talk about something else. How about your teachers? Did you like your teachers?"

"Like my teachers? Are you serious? I have no idea if I like them or not, because they kept kicking me out of class and sending me to the assistant principal's office."

"You got sent to the office? What did you do?"

"Why do you assume I did something wrong?"

She raises her eyebrows. "Well, normally that's how it works—you do something wrong, and then they send you to the office."

"Apparently, you don't have to do something wrong. Like in Spanish class, she kept correcting my Spanish over and over again. It was so aggravating. Finally I switched completely over to Spanish and asked her where she learned the language. She said the University of Wisconsin. I told her that maybe that's how they speak Spanish in Wisconsin but in South America, Europe, and the rest of the world, they speak it like I do."

Jenny bursts out laughing, then quickly pulls herself together. "Seriously? You really said that?"

"I did. I couldn't help myself."

"Cody. You have to treat your teachers with respect."

"Treat them with respect? When they try to tell me something's right and it's wrong, what am I supposed to do? Just sit there and nod my head?"

Jenny stares at me for a while. I guess she's thinking, then she takes a deep breath and in an overly calm voice asks, "Cody . . . how many times did you get sent to the office?"

"Including the time the security guard dragged me there?"

Her eyes blink for a while. It reminds me of a radio searching for a signal. "Yes . . . including the security guard."

"Four times."

"Four times? Are you *kidding* me? Who gets sent to the office *four times*?"

"I guess I do."

Jenny shakes her head and starts up the Jeep. I can tell she's mad. We drive to the cottage in silence. I think I'd prefer if she yelled. She turns on the radio and it plays soft and low like a movie soundtrack.

I stare out the window and wonder what my dad's doing right now. I look at my watch; he's probably having a late lunch. We used to have the best lunches together. Restaurants would treat us like royalty. My dad has this great way of talking to people; he could thread a needle with words if he had to.

Even in a crowded restaurant you would think we were the only people in the room. The waiters and waitresses would fall all over us but I guess my dad's generosity might have had something to do with that. People like to say that money talks. Well, my dad knows how to make it shout.

There's this darkness now, this emptiness that surrounds me, and I can feel it slowly seeping into my skin. The longer I'm away from my dad the thicker this emptiness becomes. None of this would be happening to me if we were still together. Doesn't he know there are other things in this world that can kill you besides bombs and bullets?

Try spending forty-five minutes in Mr. Stanton's algebra class. Now *that's* lethal. It should come with a warning.

The Jeep pulls into the driveway and stops by the garage. Jenny turns off the engine and the music dies with it.

I'm about to move but something stops me: a thought that's been burning away in my head.

"Aunt Jenny."

"Yes."

"What was my mother like?"

I think the question caught her off guard. She seems hesitant, unsure, like a diver frozen at the end of a very high diving board thinking about a difficult jump.

"She was . . . a lot like me but completely different. I always lacked confidence, but not Jodi. She excelled at everything she did. She was athletic, popular, and always did well in school. She was a fantastic sister. I loved and admired her so much."

Jenny stares through the windshield for a moment. "I guess you could say she was like this great, strong, mighty ship. Her only fault was when it came time to raise a sail she always left that to others and the sails they cast were never large enough to pull her along."

"What do you mean by that?"

Jenny puts her keys into her purse before giving me a sad smile. "I mean your mom was a strong, intelligent woman. If she had lived, I believe she would have done some incredible things in this world."

"You really think so?"

"I know it. Actually, you remind me of her."

I'd been studying my backpack. I look up into her eyes. "I do? How?"

"You have her determination, her intelligence, and her smile."

"Really? She smiled like me?"

"She sure did. When I see you smile it brings back so many pleasant memories."

We head over to the cottage. I quickly change, grab a water bottle, and go outside. A few days ago I took a bunch of thick, old cushions from discarded lawn chairs and wrapped them around a tree by the side of the cottage. I secured them with a ton of duct tape, and it turned out to be a really good kick bag.

All I want to do now is knock the stuffing out of those cushions for a while and forget all about this day. I'll start with a hundred high front kicks and move on from there.

I think about Cell Phone Girl.

Bam, bam, smack, bam!

I think about Steroid Steve.

Bam, smack, bam, bam!

I think about the Ice Queen, Mrs. Owens, and her "low tolerance for troublemakers."

Bam, bam, bam, smack!

I think about that dumb locker I couldn't get open. I know how to hot-wire cars, pick locks, and bypass the best security systems money can buy, but I get stumped by a stupid junior high combination lock.

Bam, bam, bam, smack, smack!

That Spanish teacher.

Bam, bam, bam, smack.

The English teacher.

Bam, smack, bam, bam.

The terrible food they served for lunch.

Bam, bam, smack!

The way everyone made fun of my clothes.

Bam, smack, bam, bam.

My mother. Why was she taken from me? Why couldn't she have lived? I can feel the tears of frustration starting to flow down my cheek.

Bam, bam, smack, smack.

I hate this.

Bam, smack, bam, bam.

It's so stupid.

I hear a deep voice behind me. "If you lower your shoulder you'll get greater height and force on that kick."

Out of the corner of my eye I can see Andy. How long has he been standing there? I turn my back to him and quickly wipe my face.

I bury my emotions and follow his suggestion, lowering my shoulder, but it doesn't seem to change anything.

"No, no, no. That's too low. Here, turn around. I'll show you."

I turn around and face Andy. He's wearing gray sweats and a T-shirt that says ARMY across the front. A tan, socklike thing covers his stump. If he noticed I was crying he doesn't let on.

"Here, you lower your shoulder like this."

He shows me what he means and I can immediately see how it would be helpful.

Then he sets his feet at a slight angle. "Now, this is what I want you to do: kick me in the chin."

"You want me to kick you in the chin?"

He chuckles. "Well, I want you to *try* to kick me in the chin. Don't worry, I'm a martial-arts instructor, I'll move."

"Are you sure?"

"Yes."

I bow to him just like my dad taught me to. He smiles and bows back to me.

I get in my stance. "Okay. Are you ready?"

"I'm ready when you are."

I kick him in the chin. He falls backward onto the grass.

Jenny bursts out of the cottage, and shouts, "Cody! What in the world is wrong with you? Why did you kick Andy?"

"He asked me to."

She runs to my side and the two of us look down at Andy. He's rubbing his chin and shaking his head. He grins up at me. "Man, for a little guy you sure pack a big wallop."

Jenny kneels by his side. "Andy, are you okay? I'm sorry. I don't know what's wrong with Cody."

He sits up and starts to laugh. "There's nothing wrong with Cody. He's right, I asked him to kick me. I just didn't realize he was that quick. I guess he's full of surprises."

Andy slowly rises to his feet and then gives me a bow. "Here's a very valuable lesson—I'm glad I was able to demonstrate it for you: *Never* underestimate your opponent."

IMPORT AND EXPORT

"Cody, I want to show you something."

We head over to Andy's basement. I'm thinking he wants to show me something from the army: a souvenir, a photo album, or maybe even a weapon. When he opens the door I can feel the smile stretch across my face. It's a room full of exercise equipment.

There are karate bags, weight and aerobic machines, free weights, and thick mats covering every inch of the floor. It's a midsize gym that rivals some of the best health clubs I've ever seen.

"Wow, this is amazing!"

He laughs as we walk into the room but there's something sad about the sound. There's no true joy behind it. "I guess you can say I'm a bit of a compulsive. Most guys would be happy with a weight bench and a few weights, but I've always got to take everything to the extreme."

I move around the room; there's equipment here that I've never even seen before.

"I can't believe this."

"I've spent a lot of time and money putting this together. I guess it's . . . maybe it's too much. I don't know, sometimes I think I would have been better off just messing with a car or something like that. Hey, check this out." Andy opens a closet, reaches in, and a moment later music is pumping into the room. I look around and notice recessed speakers built into the walls and ceiling. The sound is rich and full.

I ease into a hydraulic leg press machine, check the pressure gauge setting, and begin pushing the plate forward in long, slow movements. "This place is great. My dad always said, if you're going to do something, do it the best you possibly can."

"Sounds like your dad likes things to be perfect."

A short laugh escapes; it just pops out of my mouth like a shotgun shell. "Oh man, that's an understatement."

He gives me an odd look. "Looks like I touched a nerve."

I stare at my feet resting on the plate. "What? No. It's just that with his job it's important that things are . . . um, done perfectly the first time."

"What kind of work does your father do?"

I follow our standard response to this question. "He's in the import-export business. It's important that he pay attention to the details."

"What does he import and export?"

"Mainly electronics, computers, televisions, um . . . lamps, you know, that kind of stuff."

He's still looking at me. "The import-export business, huh? Funny, I once went into Pakistan using that as a cover. I don't think we really fooled anyone. I could have used some advice from your father."

I want to change the subject. I don't like the way this is going. I feel like I'm balancing on top of my words. I'm worried if I pile them too high they'll all slip out from under me. Without thinking I blurt out, "What about your father? Where does he live?"

He doesn't say anything at first, just walks over to a rack of dumbbells and picks up one of the midsize weights. He curls it a few times; I notice that his small stump moves upward with the movement of his good arm. It looks like a dog's wagging tail.

It occurs to me that his father might have died. Sometimes I say the stupidest things. My dad always told me to think before I speak.

After about ten curls he says, "My dad disappeared."

"He disappeared? What do you mean . . . disappeared?"

He drops his weight back on the rack and grabs another heavier one and continues curling. "When Albert was four months old, I was about your age, maybe a little younger. Everything seemed fine, everyone seemed happy. Then one day my dad went off to work and never came home."

"What happened to him?"

He drops his weight back on the rack, this time more forcefully than the last. There's a loud, metallic clang. "Nobody knows. It used to drive me crazy, the not knowing. Sometimes I think he just left us, went off someplace and started a brand-new life. Other times I think something terrible must have happened to him, maybe he picked up a bad hitchhiker or stopped to help the wrong person. I don't know."

I decrease the machine's pressure and it hisses loudly, then I press the plate out a few more times. "So you never heard from him again?"

"That's right. Not a word, a letter, or even an e-mail."

I guess I should let it drop but I'm really curious; it's my nature. "Did the police look for him?"

"In the beginning we talked to them but I don't think they looked very hard. They seemed to have it in their heads that he left us."

"Do you?"

"Do I what?"

Andy reaches up to a chin-up bar and pulls himself up a few times with his one arm.

"Do you think he left you guys?"

He drops back to the mat and blows out a breath. "Well, one

way or another he left us. Right? The effect is the same, regardless of the reason."

"Did you ever hire a private investigator?"

He gives me a look that I recognize. It's the look you give someone when they're asking way too many questions. I get off the leg press machine and move over to a box of karate weapons and start sifting through it. I'm surprised when he starts talking again.

"A few years ago I was with military intelligence. I ran a check on my dad: name, social security number, bank accounts, driver's license, passport applications, everything I could think of. It all came up blank. He just . . . disappeared."

"That's weird, like a movie or something. How did Albert deal with it?"

Andy shakes his head. I can tell he really doesn't want to talk about this anymore. I start thinking about new things to talk about, maybe karate or the army. I feel like a jerk for asking so many stupid questions.

I almost jump when he starts talking again. "Albert didn't know anything different. Our life without Dad was his normal. I was his older brother, almost like a father, and his mother was just another struggling single mom. I think there were times when it was tough for him. Sometimes we'd talk about it all and I'd try to tell him . . ."

Andy stops talking. I turn around and notice Albert standing by the door. He's got a strange expression on his face.

"Hey, we're going into town later. Mom wants to know if you need anything."

"No. I think I'm all set."

"Okay, well, if you think of anything we're leaving in about an hour. Oh, she baked some cookies, too. They're on the kitchen counter."

Albert turns and starts to walk away.

"Get back here!"

"Yeah?"

Andy seems aggravated. "Why didn't you say hello to Cody?"

He shrugs. "Dunno, just didn't, no big deal."

"It *is* a big deal. Don't be rude. Say hello to Cody and tell him you're sorry."

"Hey, Cody. Sorry about that."

"That's okay."

Andy walks over to Albert. "Why don't you come in and we'll get a quick workout together."

"I dunno, I've kinda got some homework and stuff."

Andy places his arm around his little brother's shoulders and leads him into the room. "Come on, it's early, you can do your homework later. I was going to show some karate moves to Cody. I could use your help."

He looks at me. "Albert's been studying karate since he was about six. He's a member of the dojo in town."

It doesn't take much more talking to get Albert to join us.

The three of us go at it together for about forty minutes. Albert surprises me. He's in great shape and really knows his karate. He doesn't seem to grasp my level of experience, but that's okay. I let him show me moves I've known for years and I don't get offended when he tries to "correct" me.

In the end it's Andy who tires first. I grab three bottles of water from the small refrigerator in the corner. We head outside and sit in lawn chairs under a large tree.

Andy takes the cold water bottle and rolls it across his forehead. His shirt is soaked through with sweat and he suddenly seems very tired. "Man, I'm still not anywhere near one hundred percent yet. I guess getting blown up takes a lot out of you."

For a passing second I almost tell them about the café bombing but realize that's a box that can't be closed once it's opened. There's a tall wall of secrets that will always surround me.

Andy stretches out on his chair, takes a long pull from his water bottle, and looks my way. "You know something? I never asked you about your first day of school. How was it? Any problems?"

"It was . . . um, it wasn't really what I expected. I'm sure it will get better once I get used to it. I've got gym tomorrow. I've never been to a gym class before. That should be fun."

Albert laughs. "Don't count on it. Coach Dinatelli can be a real pain."

Andy leans forward. "So school was kind of tough? What, the kids or the teachers?"

"Both. It's all so new and different to me. I don't know how to fit in with the other kids or how to talk to the teachers without making them mad. I don't even know what to wear. How pathetic is that?"

Andy smiles. "Don't know what to wear? That one seems easy to correct. Tell you what. Why don't you go into town with Albert? I'm sure he can hook you up with some good clothes. What do you say, Al, can you help Cody out?"

He smiles. "Sure, why not. I could use a couple new shirts myself."

CAMOUFLAGE

No one laughs as I walk down the hall. There's no pointing or new nicknames. I don't hear anyone calling me "Mr. Shorty Shorts." Cell phone cameras are not snapping my picture; hushed voices are not mocking me.

I guess I've found the required costume. Special thanks go out to Albert. I am now officially dressed for the junior high experience. I blend right in. I feel camouflaged.

I'm walking past a huge mirror. There's a sign above it that reads ARE YOU LOOKING AT AN HONOR STUDENT? I stop and study my reflection. What comes to mind is "I'm looking at a stranger." The long, baggy shorts, oversize T-shirt, baseball cap, and brightly colored sneakers might be what everyone else is wearing, but this isn't me. I feel like an impostor. I'm used to my custom-fitted suits and designer ties. I'm used to expensive leather belts and highly polished shoes. How am I ever going to get used to dressing like this?

Albert appears by my side and lightly punches my shoulder. "Hey."

"Hey."

He eyes my reflection and the expression on my face. "Come on. The clothes look great."

"I guess."

He lowers his voice. "We've been over and over this. You look sharp. The clothes fit you fine. Relax."

"I know. It's just that I'm not used to dressing like this, that's all."

Albert rolls his eyes. "Yeah, well, just try to loosen up, okay? You're walking around like you stole your clothes out of somebody's locker."

"Okay, I'll try."

"Gotta run. History with Mrs. Smith."

He takes off, then stops and turns around. "Hey, what's your next class?"

I smile. It's the class I've been looking forward to all morning. "Gym."

He shakes his head. "Well . . . good luck. Don't say I didn't warn you. Oh, what lunch period do you have, A or B?"

"B."

"Me too. Look for me . . . I'll save you a seat. Okay?"

"Okay."

I head for the gym but go down the wrong hall and wind up at the girls' gym. I find my way to the right gym just as the bell rings.

A tall, dark-haired man wearing gray sweats and a Yankees baseball cap is standing in the gym with a couple students. His muscular arms are folded across his chest.

He looks up as I walk into the room and bellows, "May I help you?"

"Um, I'm new. My name's Cody Saron. Here's my paperwork."

I walk over and hand him the form. He handles himself like an army drill sergeant.

"You're late."

"Sorry, like I said, I'm new. It took me a while to find the right gym."

He studies the form in his hand. "There's no excuse for being late. Do you hear me?"

"Yes."

"Yes, what?"

"Um, yes, sir."

"You will refer to me at all times as either Coach or Coach Dinatelli. Do you hear me?"

"Yes, sir."

He stares at me, clearly aggravated.

"I mean, yes sir, Coach."

He whistles and shakes his head. "Wow, I've been warned about your attitude and I'm telling you right here and now: I will not—I *do* not—tolerate insubordination. I hope you're hearing me. Do you know what insubordination means?"

"Yes, sir."

He's suddenly incredibly angry. He looks like he's about to grab me and throw me against the wall. He moves his face inches away from mine and shouts, "Yes, sir, what?"

The other kids in the room are just standing there, not daring to move or talk. I can tell they're all terrified. There's something obviously wrong with this guy. If he touches me, I'm going to head butt him, sweep his left knee, quickly break his right arm, and put him down hard. I'm not going to risk him getting up again.

I meet his gaze and stare him right in the eye. Very calmly and deliberately I reply, "Yes . . . sir . . . Coach."

He smiles slightly and nods his head. "Okay . . . I see how this is going to play out. Do you have a school-issued gym uniform and a lock?"

I'm caught off guard by his quick change of attitude and the question. "Um, well, I've got a lock, shorts, and a T-shirt . . . Coach."

"A school-issued uniform?"

"Um, no. I didn't realize I needed one. I thought just a T-shirt and shorts would be okay . . . Coach."

"Didn't you read the handbook?"

I remember staring at Renee Carrington while Miss DeNitto plowed through it. "I kind of skimmed it . . . Coach."

He shakes his head and looks up toward the ceiling. Then he turns to the kids standing next to us and sarcastically says, "He skimmed it. Did you hear that? He *skimmed* it. I guess he's just too busy to read it properly."

They nervously laugh with the coach until he points at a tall skinny kid. "Pogo Stick, tell Mr. Saron what happens when you forget your uniform."

Pogo Stick seems embarrassed at having to be the bearer of bad news. "Uh, the coach has a couple girl uniforms. He makes you wear one of those."

Great.

After the coach gives me the uniform, assigns me a locker, and I change, I'm the last one out of the locker room. I go outside to join the rest of the class. There's about thirty of them and they're all sitting on the grass. The coach is marching back and forth in front of them, holding a football in his hand.

As I walk out the door in my baby blue uniform with its pink trim, he yells, "Run, Saron! Nobody walks in my class!"

I run over to the group. A big kid with a face full of pimples and long greasy hair shouts, "Nice uniform!" The class starts to laugh.

The coach tucks the football under his arm and blows his whistle. "Listen up, everybody! This is Miss Cody Saron. She'll be in our class from now on. She's been going to a private school in jolly old England. Everybody say hello to our new Teacup."

The class shouts, "Hello, Teacup!"

Great.

The coach points at an overweight kid in the front row. "Frankfurter!"

He lumbers to his feet. "Yes, Coach?"

"You know the drill. Lap time—one full lap around the field. We'll give you a head start and if the whole class passes you, you'll have to take another lap. If you can beat anyone in the class, you can rest while the class takes another lap. You ready, Frank-furter?"

The large boy sighs heavily. "Yes, Coach."

He blows his whistle and shouts, "Okay, go!"

Frankfurter starts plodding along. He's incredibly slow. It almost looks like he's running underwater.

Coach turns his attention back to the class. He starts tossing the ball from one hand to the other. "Okay. Anybody care to guess what we'll be playing today?"

Someone up front ventures, "Football?"

"Yes, Sherlock. Football. Specifically flag football. Count off by twos."

He points at someone in the front and the guy calls out "One!"

the guy next to him shouts, "Two!" and then the following guy yells, "Three!"

Coach angrily throws the football at the guy who said "three." It bounces off his leg. "I said by twos! That's 'one, two; one, two; one, two!' I can't believe this. Did you guys all have bowls of stupid for breakfast this morning?"

We quickly count off. I'm a two.

The whistle sounds again, and he points at a couple boxes. "Now collect your belts and flags. The ones will be wearing white flags and the twos red. After you secure your belts and flags, take a lap. Remember, if everyone doesn't pass Frankfurter you all have to take a second lap. Tell Frankfurter he's a red, which is kind of funny, if you think about it."

I almost forgot about Frankfurter. I look for him and see him about halfway around the field. I can't believe he's only made it that far. Even though it doesn't seem possible, it looks as if he's actually running slower than before.

One by one we collect our flags and belts, and take off like bees leaving the hive.

Frankfurter is about three quarters of the way around the field when the first runner passes him. He calls out to Frankfurter, "You're red!" The next fifteen or so runners also tell him he's red. When I'm about to pass him, I glance his way. He's breathing hard and sweating.

"You okay?"

He croaks, "Yeah."

"You sure?"

"Yeah."

A number of runners pass us. They each call out, "You're red!" I continue to run next to Frankfurter. I can't bring myself to pass him.

"My name's Cody."

He has a hard time replying but manages to spit out the words. My . . . name's . . . Frank."

"Has anyone ever lost one of these races to you?"

"Nope."

"So you always run two laps?"

"Yup."

I smile. "Today, you're only going to run one."

He looks at me in disbelief. "Don't do . . . that. The class . . . will . . . hate you."

I motion at the rest of the pack with my chin. "Those guys? They were all just laughing at me and calling me Teacup. They deserve to take another lap."

"Coach will be . . . ticked off . . . big-time."

I snicker. "Yeah, I know."

Frank looks my way. A smile starts to spread across his face. "I think things . . . are going to get . . . a lot more . . . interesting around here."

The two of us plod along toward the finish line. I make sure

Frank's always a step or two in front of me. The closer to the finish line we get the louder the class's taunts grow.

I glance over at the coach and his face is etched with barely suppressed rage.

There's silence when Frank crosses the line first. Everyone looks over at the coach expecting an explosive reaction. We see the fire in his eyes. We see the clenching of his jaw and fists but we don't hear the yelling and screaming that was expected.

He points at Frank. "Take a seat."

Coach blows his whistle, then shouts, "Everybody else up! Apparently Teacup wants you all to take another lap, so get moving."

There's a collective groan. Then runners start flying from the hive once again. When I pass the coach he points at me. "Teacup, since you like running so much, you can take three laps."

When I finish my laps I join the red team. They're walking toward the end of the field, getting ready to receive a kickoff.

The coach jogs over to my side and starts yelling into my ear. "Teacup, you realize this is American football. Not soccer. Right?"

I look straight ahead. "Yes, Coach."

"Do you know how to play American football?"

"Yes, Coach."

"This is flag football, which means you do not—I repeat, do not—tackle your opponent. You just grab his flag. Do you under-stand?"

"Yes, Coach."

He looks around at the other kids. "Let's see what the little Teacup can do. Try not to break him, okay? I hear teacups are fragile."

The teams line up for the kickoff and a few moments later I'm watching the ball sail through the air, tumbling end over end toward me. I catch it cleanly and quickly dodge to the side to avoid having someone grab my flag. Then I dodge and weave across the field, easily avoiding everyone who attempts to grab one of my flags. It's all the same moves I use in karate.

When I'm about ten yards from the goal line I stop and place the ball in the arms of one of the opposing players. He runs about ten feet before someone pulls one of his flags.

Coach runs onto the field, blowing his whistle and shouting, "Teacup! What's wrong with you? I thought you said you know how to play this game. The goal line's over there."

He's frantically pointing at the goal line.

"Sorry, Coach."

I let the other team run a few plays and move down the field before I intercept a pass. Once again I easily dodge and weave my way within ten yards of the goal line before placing the ball in another opponent's arms.

This time Coach's whistle sounds like an ear-piercing scream. He shouts, "Teacup, I know what you're doing! Take two more laps!"

I run the laps and rejoin my team. They're all in a huddle. I'm sweating and breathing heavily as I squeeze in with them. The quarterback's grinning. "Hey, Teacup, if I give you the ball are you going to do the same thing with it?"

"The name's Cody, and yeah, probably."

He shakes his head. "Coach will go ballistic. You know that, don't you?"

"Yes."

There's suppressed laughter all around me.

"Sounds like a good play to me. You sure you want to do that?"

"Yes."

Frank's giggling loudly.

"Okay, then. Let's light this fuse and see what happens. Break huddle on three."

We all chant together. "One, two, three!" Then we clap our hands and line up.

The quarterback takes the snap and laterals the ball over to me. I'm about to start running when I get a new idea. Standing over by the coach is one of my opponents. I throw the ball to him, a perfect spiral that lands right in his hands. He runs down the field for a touchdown.

Moments later I'm back in the hall, passing the huge mirror with its sign ARE YOU LOOKING AT AN HONOR STUDENT? I glance at my reflection. I'm still dressed in the girls' baby blue gym uniform with pink trim. Coach Dinatelli is hauling me by my arm to the assistant principal's office. He looks insanely angry, almost to the point of appearing comical.

Everyone stops to watch us. I struggle to keep my expression blank and to keep up with the coach's quick pace. I could be wrong, but I seriously doubt this is what an honor student looks like.

DAMAGED
BUT NOT BROKEN

A red-tailed hawk circles overhead. I stand at the bus
stop and watch. It soars like a small, deadly kite.

Cell Phone Girl watches me for a second and then mutters,
"Head case."

I mutter, "Barnacle brain," then watch her teeter up the street
in her exceedingly high heels, her thumbs dancing across her cell
phone, surely sending mindless text messages to her masses.

I scan the sky, looking for my hawk, but it's nowhere to
be found. I sling my backpack over my shoulder and head for
home.

It's not a long walk, but it feels like one with this heavy pack.
This morning Albert walked with me and even though we didn't

talk much I enjoyed the company. He told me he doesn't take the bus home after school, he does something else. Maybe it's wrestling, or could it be band practice? I don't remember. I wasn't really paying attention.

I wonder what my dad was like when he was my age. Did he walk to school with a friend? Was he popular? Did he have to carry his books in a backpack? My dad and I lived in a quiet little bubble. He never talked about his past. Now he's not around but I'm still living inside this bubble; it's become part of my skin. I wish I could shed my skin like a snake.

"Cody."

I look over. Andy's standing in the shadows of his garage. I'm surprised I didn't see him right away. I've got to remember to stay focused. I can't drift around in a pathetic fog all day. I walk toward him and he joins me in the driveway. He's wearing a suit, but what really catches my attention is his arm.

"Hey, you're wearing your arm."

He looks at it and starts moving it around. "Yeah, but this isn't the good one. This one's more cosmetic than anything else. I'm still trying to get used to the good one. It's surprisingly heavy, like carrying a small weight around all day."

I'm so used to seeing him with a missing arm that it actually seems strange to me. Somehow by adding this new part it subtracts something from the whole.

I just nod my head like I know exactly what he's talking about.

His mood changes and he suddenly seems very uncomfortable. "Hey, I was wondering . . . I was hoping you could do me a huge favor."

"Sure, at least I think so. What do you need?"

"I've got this job interview and, well, this is kind of embarrassing. Do you know how to tie a tie? I can't seem to do it with only one working arm and my mother isn't around to lend a helping hand."

Somehow he seems to shrink with the confession.

I try to act casual. "Sure, no problem. I've been tying my own tie since I was nine."

He's got the tie draped loosely around his neck. I put down my backpack, stand in front of him, and attempt to tie it. After two or three frustrating minutes, I have to confess, "Sorry, this is really tough. I'm not used to doing it like this. It's all backward. Maybe we should find a mirror. That's how my dad used to tie my tie. He'd stand behind me and use the mirror."

"Sounds good. There's a mirror in the bathroom. You can stand on the edge of the tub to reach over my shoulders."

A car horn honks a few times on the street.

We both look over and see a dark blue convertible slowly driving by the front of the house. It's fantastic—a totally restored car from thirty or forty years ago, big, hulky, and flashy in a way that's completely different from today's cars. The sun is gleaming off the highly polished hood and the engine is rumbling with suppressed power.

The top is down, and behind the wheel there's a woman with long brown hair waving at us. She's smiling, and even from this distance it's easy to see how incredibly beautiful she is.

She pulls the massive car into the driveway. Andy breathes in sharply. I glance his way and he looks both nervous and excited. He's smiling, but the smile seems a lot like his suit, something he just put on to make a good impression.

The car slowly cruises down the driveway and comes to a stop next to us. The music is pounding and the woman's smile seems to grow as large as the music is loud. A moment later she reaches down, turns the key, and a new, tight silence quickly settles around us. The only sound is the *tick, tick, tick* of the engine cooling down.

She shakes her head and says, "You know, I've used a phone with one hand before. I imagine with all your talents you could do it too."

He slowly starts to walk toward the car. "I've never been very good with phones, even the two-handed kind."

"How you doing, Andy?"

"I'm okay, Annie, damaged but not broken. How about you?"

She steps out of the car and starts walking toward him. When she's about six feet away, she laughs, runs the last few feet, and throws her arms around him.

"Oh, I can't believe it. You're really back. I've missed you. I've missed you so much."

"Missed you too. You're still the fairest one of all."

She smiles over his shoulder. "My magic mirror returns."

"Always glad to perform a public service." He glances my way. "Oh, Annie, this is Cody, he's living in the cottage. Cody, this is Annie. She's . . . an old friend."

She gives me a little wave. "Hey, Cody, nice to meet you. You keeping an eye on Andy?"

"Hi, Annie. He seems to be doing okay."

"Don't let him fool you."

Andy eyes the car. "Enough about me. How about the GTO? Does Johnny know you're driving his baby?"

"Of course he does. I wouldn't dare touch it without his say-so. You know how he is about this car. But when I told him my old VW needed a new clutch, he insisted I use it. It was strange, very un-Johnny-like, if you know what I mean."

"You're right. That doesn't sound like the Johnny we know."

"Yeah, he's different. I think it's the . . . well, did you see him at all over there?"

I can sense Andy growing uncomfortable; the smile is completely gone from his face. "A couple times but he was way up north, near Turkey, and I was mainly in Baghdad."

"When you saw him how did he look?"

"He . . . he looked good, I guess. The last time I saw him was about five months ago. There's a club on the base. It's a good place for music and something cold to drink on a hot night. We went there and spent most of our time together talking about all the crazy things the three of us used to do."

Her smile loses its conviction of happiness. "Yeah, those were good times, real good times. It seems so long ago now."

She glances at her watch. "Oh, speaking of time. How did that happen? I'm late. I'm sorry. I've gotta go. I have to pick up my little sister."

She gives him another big hug. "Welcome home, hero. Call me. Okay? Seriously, I mean it. We'll go out and catch up."

"You bet."

We watch the car back out of the driveway, toot its horn, and then roar away in a cloud of dust and exhaust.

Andy and I stand together in silence. We can hear the car fading away into the distance, the sound of its engine growing dimmer with each passing moment. He seems upset and I don't want to say anything that might upset him further. So I just stand there, waiting for him to say something. If I had the power to fade away from Andy like the sound of that engine, I think that's what I would choose to do right now.

Finally he turns my way and forces a smile. "Hey, how about helping me with this stupid tie?"

"Sure."

We walk in silence through his house and into a bathroom. Andy faces the mirror, and I stand on the edge of the bathtub behind him. I reach around his wide shoulders, look in the mirror and start to tie his tie. It's definitely easier this way.

I search for something to say. I can feel the silence thickening around us. I blurt out, "Um, Annie's real nice. Did you guys used to date or something?"

He seems aggravated by the question. "No. What gave you that idea?"

"I guess the way she hugged you."

"She's been seeing Johnny for as long as I can remember. Johnny and I joined the service together. He used to be my best friend."

"Used to be?"

"Still is, I guess. I just haven't seen him in a while."

"Why?"

"We were stationed hundreds of miles apart, that's all."

"I thought best friends keep in touch."

"Yeah, well, sometimes they don't. Okay?"

I finish with his tie. "How's that look?"

He eyes it for a second. "Perfect."

I step down off the tub and nearly fall when a loose, round rug slips out from under me. I steady myself on Andy's shoulder and then follow him outside.

I squint as we walk into the glare of the afternoon sun. Somehow it seems brighter than just a few minutes ago.

A deep voice barks, "You guys call a cab?"

I'm startled by the voice and I flinch.

There's a taxi waiting in the driveway. The driver's leaning against the roof. I can't believe I didn't hear the car pull up to the house. Why did it take me so long to notice it? I'm slipping, getting soft, not paying attention; I'm being conquered from within. Time to get my head back in the game before something happens.

Andy looks at me and shakes his head. "Sometimes I know exactly what you're thinking. I'm not sure what I find more disturbing—that I know what you're thinking, or that I'm thinking the same thoughts." He waves at the driver. "Yeah, I called. Sorry, I didn't hear you pull up."

The driver snorts. "No problem. I just got here." But judging from the look on his face I'm guessing it *is* a problem. This guy looks like he would have a problem waiting an extra ten seconds for his passenger to shut the door.

Andy pats me on the back. "Thanks for the hand. Wish me luck."

"Good luck."

When I open the door to the cottage, Jenny is standing a few feet away, waiting for me, clutching her cell phone. She seems very anxious. I quickly glance around the room expecting the worst.

"What's the matter?"

"Where have you been?"

"Um, school. You know, that place I go to five days a week."

"Don't be a smart-aleck. You should have been home at least a half hour ago."

I smile. Is this what it's like to have a mother worrying about me? "Andy asked me to help him with something. What's the big deal?"

Her cell phone goes off, she glances at it. There's a change to her expression: it's all business now.

She quickly hands me the phone and starts talking as fast as she can. "Okay, it's your father. He called earlier. You can talk for one minute, not one second more. He said you'd understand."

I do. I fumble with the phone before I manage to open it. I nervously place it against my ear.

"Hello?"

"Cody, is that you?" The connection is poor and I can hear heavy equipment in the background. It sounds like a large steel wheel grinding boulders into pebbles.

"Dad?"

"Yes, it's me. How are you, son?"

"I'm okay. Where are you? It sounds like you're inside a coffee grinder."

"I can't say. Do you understand why?"

"Yes, I understand." I press the phone closer to my ear in an effort to hear better. I can feel my heart starting to pound.

"Cody, I love you. I want you to know that."

"I love you too. Is everything okay?"

"Yes. I'm just busy taking care of our little problem. Hopefully I'll have it settled soon and we can be together again."

"How long will it take?"

"I have no way of knowing that, son. You're just going to have to be patient."

"Okay."

"How's school? Was everything okay with the transcripts?"

I start to laugh. "Everything was fine, but why did you add that 'problem with authority' thing? It's really giving me problems with authority."

I can hear him chuckling. "I wanted them to keep you on your toes and press you to work harder. I guess it's working."

"Well, they definitely have me on my toes."

There's a moment of awkward silence. We can both sense that the minute is about to expire. There's no meaning in the silence, it's just a complete lack of sound.

He starts talking faster. "Our time's almost up. Take care of yourself. Remember: Always stay diligent. Don't forget, your eyes are your most important weapon. Always expect the unexpected. Listen to Jenny; don't give her a hard time. Study hard. I love you, Cody."

"I love you too. Oh, and Dad . . . ," The phone goes dead in my hand. I stand there listening to the silence for a while, unable to accept that the conversation's over. I can feel the heavy fog of emptiness settling around me. I inhale it deeply. I can't help myself.

One minute. That's all I got, just one lousy minute. One minute isn't long enough for a conversation; it's barely long enough to ask for directions. I could hold my breath longer than a minute. I think this whole "international man of mystery" routine stinks. It really does. Why couldn't my dad have been an accountant?

Jenny places her hand on my shoulder. "Is everything okay?"

I look into her eyes. There's so much concern there; she really does care for me. Part of me feels like falling into her arms and crying against her shoulder and the other part is completely repulsed by the weakness of the idea.

I'm not sure what to do with these feelings. It's like they're in a washing machine, spinning around, mixing together like socks, shirts, and underwear. I can't just reach in and take only what I need.

I mumble, "Yeah, I guess."

"How's your dad?"

"Fine, I guess, but who knows? I'm sick of all this. I'm going to my room."

"Sure, okay. Hey, do you want me to make you some hot chocolate? It's really good."

"No, thanks."

I walk down the hall and into my room, then close the door

and fall upon my bed. I feel as empty as my walls. I bury my head in the pillow; my eyes start to water. I don't know what's wrong with me.

Knock.

Knock.

Knock.

Jenny's voice is soft and low, filled with concern. "Cody, it's me . . . can we talk?"

I sit up in my bed. "Just a sec." I wipe my eyes with my sleeve and slowly walk across the room. I'm at the door but I just can't bring myself to open it. I lean against it instead.

"What do you want?"

Her voice is like a feather. "I just want to talk, that's all. Open the door."

I'm tempted, but I can't. "Not now. Later, okay?"

"Cody, I want to help you. Talk to me, maybe I'll understand."

"I can't. I just want to be left alone."

There's a long moment of silence. Then she says, "You don't have to open the door. Just talk to me."

I slide down to the floor and sit with my elbows on my knees, hands on the sides of my face. I stare off across the room, focusing on nothing.

A little while later I hear a noise in the hall and realize it's Jenny sliding down to the floor. I picture her sitting out there, her back just inches behind mine on the other side of the door.

Time slips away. The world moves forward while I just sit here. The emptiness is like a weight pressing down on top of me. I doubt I could stand even if I tried.

I hear a car pull into the driveway, then the sound of a door opening. A minute later, I hear Andy saying good-bye. I realize it must be his taxi. Andy went to the job interview already? He's back? How long have I been sitting here? The room's a lot darker than it was before.

"You still there, Jen?"

"Yeah, hon, still here . . . you want to talk now?"

I stare at my shoes and sneakers lying on the floor. They're scattered around like bodies. I see the waitress winking at me again. I can see her face, her smile, the way she lifted her little pinkie while she poured my dad's coffee.

I clear my throat. The words flow out of my mouth like water from a broken pipe. I've got no control over them; they're rushing to be free. My voice sounds strange, almost like it's not mine.

"Me and my dad were at this café in Santiago . . ."

I tell her the whole story, everything I can remember. When I get to the end, to the part where I find the waitress lying next to me, my voice starts to crack, and before I even know what's happening I'm crying, crying like I haven't cried in years.

I feel the door being pushed with gentle force against my

back and I give in to it. A moment later Jenny is sitting next to me, tears flowing down her face. She holds me tight; her hands are rubbing and patting my back. I close my eyes and sink into her.

For the moment, I feel safe and warm.

EYES

When I first looked into Renee Carrington's eyes—those big, beautiful brown eyes—I realized I had to spend as much time as possible with her. Whenever Mrs. Smith says something stupid or misguided I've learned to just let it slide so I can spend more time next to this special girl.

I discreetly watch her every move. I listen to her conversations with her friend Fiona. I study her extensive doodles, her colorful clothes, and focus on her odd comments in class. Like when Mrs. Smith asked her to explain the importance of the free press in a democratic society and she said, "It's like having a menu that lets you know what every restaurant in town is serving."

I notice the different ways she styles her hair, holds her pen, and taps her fingers on her desk like she's playing an invisible piano. I notice that she laughs at things the rest of the class doesn't find funny, gets sad about stuff nobody seems to care about, and is excited by what others find boring.

For the last week I've spent most of my time in class thinking about the best way to talk to her. Should I just introduce myself? Ask her about homework? Give her something? Write her a note? Hack into her computer? Everything I come up with feels really lame. I blame my clothes. They say clothes make the man; well these clothes make me feel like an insecure, tongue-tied boy. I miss my suits. I always felt confident wearing a suit.

The bell rings and another opportunity to talk to her seems to be slipping away. I can almost feel the floor moving beneath me. She's walking out the door with a quick, purposeful stride.

I pick up my books as another wave of disappointment washes over me. I wish I could talk to her. What's wrong with me? It has to be the clothes. These baggy, pocket-crazed pants are messing with my mind. I glance at her desk. It's only a few feet away from me. It would be so easy to reach out and touch her. Why is it so hard to just talk to her?

Then I notice the notebook. Her notebook. It's on the floor next to her desk. She brought her art project to class today; it's some kind of weird kite-type thing. Between juggling the artwork and her books, it's not surprising something was left behind.

Here's my chance. I snatch it off the floor and dash toward the door after her.

"Cody."

I look over at Mrs. Smith. I don't believe it. What does she want and why does she want it *now*?

"Yes, Mrs. Smith."

She gives me a smile. "I just wanted to say that I've noticed a change in your attitude. It's nice to see that you've decided to try harder in class."

"I'm not trying any harder." I can see the clock over her shoulder and I swear that second hand is mocking me. "I'm just trying hard not to get kicked out of class."

She has a slightly puzzled look etched across her face. "I see . . . perhaps we might consider this a turning point?"

"Sure, why not." I look toward the open door. "I'm sorry, Mrs. Smith, if there's nothing else, I've really got to get going."

"That's fine, Cody, I'll see you tomorrow."

"Okay."

I hurry out the door and look for Renee. She's walking down the hall by herself.

I run after her, shouting, "Renee! Renee!"

It seems like she's the only person in the hall who doesn't hear me. Everyone is turning my way except her.

"Renee! Renee! You forgot your notebook."

I tap her on the shoulder. She jumps and quickly spins around toward me. The stick in her kite swings toward my left eye. I try to avoid it but it's moving too fast.

"Ahhh!" The pain shoots through my whole body. I clutch my eye and squat down to the floor. I can't believe it. I let my guard down. Good thing my dad wasn't here to see that. I'd be doing extra training drills for a week.

She's standing over me, pulling iPod ear buds out of her ears. I can hear the sound of faint, tinny music. "What's wrong with you?" She looks alarmed. "What are you doing?"

"You poked me in the eye with your stick."

"I did?" Her expression softens. "I'm sorry. I didn't do it on purpose."

I slowly rise to my feet, blinking my eye and trying to rub the tears away. I think it will be okay, although it still really hurts.

It's tough to talk. "I know, I guess I startled you."

"Startled? Who says 'startled'?"

"I guess when you've been maimed by a stick you tend to say words like 'startled.'"

"Did you say *tend*? Who says 'tend'? First you say 'startled,' and now 'tend.'" She gives me a huge smile and a wink. "Oh, I get it, you're from Albania, right?"

"Albania?" My head's starting to hurt. "Why would you think I'm from Albania? Are you putting me on?"

"Putting you on? What an odd phrase. But that would be fun, wouldn't it? To put someone on like you put on a new suit. Just slide inside their skin and walk around for the rest of the day. See what it's like to be them."

"Um, I guess."

"You guess? What's wrong with you? I think it would be okay for a girl to try being a guy for a day, but a guy being a girl? Now that just seems plain weird to me. You want to be a girl?"

"What? No! I didn't say that. Not that there's anything wrong with girls, it's just . . . Why are we even talking about this?"

"You brought it up."

"No, I didn't."

She shrugs her shoulders. "Okay, whatever you say."

I'm starting to get really frustrated. This isn't how I wanted things to go between us. I try my best to stay calm but I can hear the tension slipping into my voice. I wave at the people in the hall with the notebook. "I have absolutely no desire to walk around in a girl's or for that matter anyone else's skin except my own."

"Oh, I'm just playin' with you. Hey! That's my notebook! What are you doing with my notebook?"

I almost forgot about it. "Oh yeah. You forgot it under your desk. I was just returning it."

She takes it out of my hand.

A teacher standing in the hall shouts, "Move it along, people! This isn't a social club!"

She starts talking faster. "Hey, don't worry. I think you're cute. Next time you want to talk to me, just talk to me. Okay? You don't have to go around stealing my stuff to get my attention."

"I didn't steal your notebook!"

"Whatever you say. Listen, I've got to get going. Oh, by the way, my name's Renee."

"I know." I can't believe I just admitted that. "I'm Cody."

"Nice to meet you, Cody. Hey . . . I was wondering. Fiona and I need a third for the class project. You seem to know a lot about history. Would you want to work with us?"

I can't believe she's asking me. Two minutes ago I didn't think I'd even be able to talk to her, and now we'll be working together! I feel a little dizzy. Just say yes and try not to sound too overly excited. Try to act cool.

"I'd love to."

I can feel my face getting red. Why did I say "love"? What a stupid thing to say, "love." *Why* did I say that?

She smiles. "Great!"

"Oh, what's the project about?"

"France."

She starts walking down the hall.

"Renee."

She turns around.

"I didn't steal your notebook."

She flashes me a smile. "I know. I left it for you. I could tell you needed an excuse to talk to me."

I'm late. Time to bolt down the hall to the gym. I really thought gym was going to be a blast. Too bad Coach Dinatelli has to take all the enjoyment out of it. The man's a fun vampire, just sucking the fun out of everything. I bet he spends his nights dancing with snakes and sticking pins into the voodoo dolls of all good people.

The bell rings as I burst into the locker room and I nearly plow right into the evil one himself. He's abandoned his black cloak, sharp teeth, and night wings for his day uniform of gray sweats and a whistle.

"Teacup. Do my eyes deceive me? Are you late?"

"I beat the bell, Coach."

"That doesn't make you on time. I expect you to be on the floor when the bell rings, not walking into the locker room. Are you on the floor?"

"No, I'm not, Coach."

"So what does that make you?"

"I guess it makes me late, Coach. Sorry, I'll change fast."

He shakes his head in disgust. "Stop talking and start changing."

I quickly move toward my locker. Just when I'm beginning to think the coach is going to let this drop, I hear him open the door leading into the gym and bellow, "Seems like Teacup and Frank-furter both arrived late today. So you all can thank them for the extra two laps you'll be taking."

I hear a loud collective groan as I round the corner to my locker. Frank's locker is next to mine and he's standing there half dressed. He turns his back to me in an effort to hide the rolls of fat draped around his body.

I start spinning my lock combo. "Coach seems to be in a bad mood again."

Frank snorts. "He's always in a bad mood. Get used to it. Now the whole class is going to be mad at us for making them take two more laps."

"We're not making them take two laps, Coach is."

"Yeah, try telling that to the class. They'll blame us. They always do."

I open my locker and quickly pull out its contents, and I'm overwhelmed by a strong, sweet smell.

Frank notices it too. "Whoa, what's that smell? Perfume?"

I lift the uniform to my nose. "Oh yeah, it's perfume. Someone sprayed a ton of it into my locker."

As he struggles to slip his excessively large shirt over his head, Frank grumbles, "Isn't school great? Don't you just love it? It's just one humiliating moment after another."

I stand there wondering what to do. I could quickly wash everything in the sink and dry it with the hand dryer, but I don't have enough time.

I could disappear, suddenly get sick, steal someone else's clothes, or call in a bomb threat. Any one of those ideas would work but I'm betting they'd create more problems than solutions.

It looks like my only option is wearing the stinking uniform.

Frank finally gets his shirt on. I pat him on the back. "Listen, my whole locker smells. Could I squeeze my street clothes into your locker?"

"Sure, no problem, if you can find the room. Are you really going to wear that thing?"

"Looks like I've got no choice."

"Coach is going to have a field day."

I slip the shirt over my head. I can't believe how bad it smells. This is one gym class I'll definitely be taking a shower after.

Sometimes you can get yourself all worked up about something and it turns out to be nothing. Other times it turns out your fears were completely justified.

Gym class—which, for me, consists largely of just running lap after lap with breaks in between for Coach to shout and call me names—is even worse than I feared it would be.

The overpowering cloud of perfume that hangs around me makes me the most tempting target of ridicule to ever step upon a gym floor. Teacup becomes Little Miss Teacup and it isn't just Coach doing the name-calling, it's the whole class. Frank's the only one who doesn't feel compelled to insult me.

Billy Foster, the tall guy that Coach has a habit of calling Pogo Stick, seems to be the main ringleader, and I strongly suspect that he had something to do with my locker taking on its sudden, overpowering stench.

After class I take a scorching-hot shower and cover myself from head to toe with soap in an effort to wash away the foul odor. I think I managed to scrub most of it off, but I'm not sure. I've become immune to the overpowering scent. My success or failure will be judged by whoever has to sit next to me for the rest of the day.

I dry off, slip into my shorts, and head for my locker. When I round the corner I find Frank, dressed only in his underwear, surrounded by Pogo Stick and five of his friends. They're pushing him back and forth from one side of the circle to the other, laughing and chanting, "Frankfurter, Frankfurter, Frankfurter," over and over.

Frank appears to be on the verge of crying, which seems to only increase their sadistic pleasure. He's folding his arms across his flabby chest in a futile attempt to cover his exposed flesh. There's a desperate, pleading look to his eyes.

I glance over at the coach's office. It's empty. Normally he can be seen behind the large glass window that looks into our locker room. It figures that when he's truly needed he's nowhere to be found.

I approach the group. "Hey, knock it off!"

They stop pushing Frank and shift toward me. They flow around me and I soon find myself by Frank's side in the center of the circle.

Pogo Stick grins. "Look what we've got here, Little Miss Teacup running to his girlfriend's defense."

I look him in the eye. "Stop this now before someone gets hurt."

A voice behind me mockingly calls out, "*Oooh*, is Little Miss Teacup scared he's gonna get *huuuuurt*?"

The others start to laugh.

Someone pushes me toward Frank. I stop a few inches short of running into him.

"I'm warning all of you. Leave us alone and nobody will get hurt."

The guy to the left of Pogo Stick snorts. "*Oooh*, I'm scared. Little Miss Teacup says he's gonna hurt us."

The big kid, with the pimply face and long greasy hair, suddenly shoves Frank into me. The two of us painfully collide and almost crash to the floor. We briefly hold each other to avoid falling.

Pogo Stick winks at us. "Look, they're dancing. Aren't they a cute couple?"

I glare at him, pucker my lips, and kiss the air. "Don't worry, sweetheart. I'll save the last dance for you."

Both his temper and his fist are quicker than I thought they'd be. I don't have time to block his punch. I snap my head back but he still manages to graze my forehead. Someone kicks me in the back.

I let the tiger out of his cage.

It only takes a few seconds. *Legs.* My eyes pick the targets and my body follows their lead. *Knees.* It happens fast, too fast for my mind to even register what's happening. *Feet.* It's simply instinct and countless hours of training taking over. *Elbows.* The switch got switched. *Hands.* They might as well have been trying to stop a moving train with a pillow.

Frank and I stand together, surveying the fallen, groaning bodies around us. He turns to me. There's an expression of shock and confusion stretched tightly across his face.

"What happened?"

I don't know what to say. I just stand there.

"Is anyone hurt?"

I look at the bodies lying around us. Something about the way they're scattered on the floor reminds me of the café bombing. I can almost smell the explosives, the charred flesh, and the fear and desperation that hung in the air that morning.

If only the waitress hadn't winked at me. It's the memory of that last sweet act that keeps constantly slicing its way into my head. It's so unbelievably sharp. I'm powerless to stop it when it chooses to pierce its way into the present.

Frank shakes my shoulder; panic in his voice as he asks, "Should I get the nurse?"

I glance around. "No."

"I think you might have really hurt someone."

I turn to Frank. Even though he didn't do anything wrong I can hear the anger creeping into my voice. "Nobody's hurt badly. They're just stunned. If I wanted to really hurt someone I would have."

He takes a few steps backward; I see the fear in his eyes. "What *are* you?"

I watch Frank. He moves until his back is against the lockers. What am I?

What, not who—maybe that's a question I should be asking myself, too. What am I?

THE MACHINE

I can feel the steady march of impending doom. That sensation that everything's about to change drastically for the worse and you're completely powerless to prevent it. Like when you bump the edge of a table and you can't do anything except watch as the expensive vase at the other end tumbles to the floor.

Mrs. Richardson is mangling Spanish again. What else is new? I can't even concentrate enough to criticize her. I can feel the wheels of the discipline machine moving, building up speed, and heading in my direction. I know it will come. How it will come is the question.

The loudspeaker crackles to life and Mrs. Owens's shrill, slightly hysterical voice can be heard angrily shouting throughout the whole school. "If Cody Saron is in the building, have him report to my office immediately! And I mean immediately!"

The machine has arrived.

Everyone in the class falls silent and turns their attention to me. It's obvious nobody's ever been called to the office quite like this before. I've suddenly become the most interesting student to ever walk through the front door.

Mrs. Richardson looks at me over her glasses and addresses me in an overly calm and composed manner. "Cody, I think Mrs. Owens would like to see you in her office."

There's a slight smile tugging at her lips.

I slowly rise to my feet, slip my books into my backpack, and ignore the snickers around me. A new battle begins.

The kids around me start whispering, "What did you do?" and "*Oooh* . . . you're in so much trouble," and other such garbage. I ignore them.

I'm just about out of the classroom when the door opens and in marches Steroid Steve, with his attitude, self-inflated chest, and ego. "I'm supposed to escort Cody Saron to the office."

Figures. They don't even trust me to find my own way to the office.

Steroid Steve and I walk together in the long, empty hall. His rubber-soled shoes squeak loudly on the tile floor. I feel like I'm walking with a cartoon character. If I weren't so worried about what was going to happen to me, I'd laugh.

The few people we encounter stare at me like I'm a rock star . . . or an ax-murderer. I've never been either, so I'm not sure.

Steve stops abruptly and glares at me. He lifts his chin. "You know something? I knew you were trouble the very first moment I saw you. Now I hear you hurt six kids. Punks like you should be kept in cages, not schools."

I meet his eyes and glare right back at him. I could have saved myself a whole lot of aggravation if I had just laid him out on the floor that first day of school. It's almost as if he reads my mind; something in his eyes changes and he takes a step backward.

At first I'm surprised, then I shake my head in disgust. I realize what I had always suspected: he's nothing but a paper tiger. I hope the school never has to truly depend upon him for protection.

We walk the remainder of the way to the office in silence. He opens the door for me and when I pass him he mutters, "I hope they kick your butt outta school."

Mrs. Owens is waiting for me. Her face looks calm but it's clear there's a dangerous current flowing just below its serene surface. I guess she's regained her composure after that bizarre loudspeaker rant.

She nods at me. "Mr. Saron."

I nod back. "Mrs. Owens."

"Please step into my office."

I follow her into the main engine of the machine, with its

full bookshelves, drawn blinds, and comfortable leather chairs. I close the door behind me, glance at the Yankees pennant, and sink into my now-familiar seat; it once again hisses my arrival. Today, instead of a defective whoopee cushion, the hissing reminds me of an angry snake. I can practically feel it wrapping its long, thick body around me.

Mrs. Owens sits behind her highly polished desk; her manicured hands folded together on its shiny surface. She holds me in an icy stare that reveals little beyond contempt. We sit in a thick silence as I wait for her to say something.

She clears her throat. "Mr. Saron, upon our first meeting I thought I made our school's zero-tolerance for violence policy quite clear. Isn't that so?"

"Yes, ma'am."

"You do understand what zero means, don't you?"

"Yes, ma'am."

"Why don't you tell me what zero means."

"It means nothing at all."

"That's right. So if we have a policy of zero tolerance when it comes to acts of violence, what do you suppose *that* means?"

"It means what it means."

She doesn't say anything. We slip back into that thick fog of silence. I become aware of a clock ticking somewhere in the room. In the outer office, I hear the muffled voices of people talking and laughing.

Finally she says, "I want to hear *your* definition of zero tolerance."

I peer at her across the desk. It's like studying a statue. She doesn't move; she rarely blinks. I keep my hands on the arms of my chair, my chin up, my gaze holding hers. I let the moment stretch on like a piano key held down until the note fades away into silence.

When the silence feels thicker than cement I say, "I think we both know what zero tolerance means."

She continues to stare at me and starts tapping her fingernails on the desk.

Tap, tap, tap.

Tap, tap, tap.

Tap, tap, tap.

It's like her nails are dancing with the ticking of the clock. They merge and spin off into an eternal waltz.

She stops tapping. "Tell me what zero tolerance means."

I take a deep breath. "Mrs. Owens, is there a reason why you're talking to me like I'm an imbecile?"

She doesn't move or flinch; she just continues to stare at me. I'm beginning to feel like a goldfish. "Why don't you tell me about what happened in gym today."

I lean forward. "I'm glad you brought that up, because I've been thinking about filing a complaint. For some reason gym largely consists of me running laps. I have no idea why Coach

Dinatelli has singled me out for this abuse. I think it may have something to do with me having lived in England. He also insists upon calling me *Teacup*. I'm worried about the psychological scars his cruelty may leave upon me."

"Stop it!"

Mrs. Owens is suddenly standing behind her desk. That dangerous undercurrent I detected before has finally risen to the surface.

"Mr. Saron, I have had enough of your shenanigans."

"What exactly does 'shenanigans' mean? It sounds like an Irish pub."

She's quickly around her desk and for the briefest of moments it looks like she's about to hit me. Which would be just about perfect, assaulted for violating a zero-tolerance violence policy.

Instead she storms past me, opens her door, and barks, "Follow me!"

We march together through the main office. All activity freezes, conversations cease, everyone watches us. The room seems to fall into a collective coma. When we pass through the door into the hall I hear the room slowly coming back to life behind us.

Mrs. Owens is walking quickly. I have to lengthen my stride just to keep up with her. If she were moving any faster I'd have to break into something between speed walking and a jog.

I follow her into the nurse's office. Mrs. Casey, the school nurse, quickly stands up. It's obvious that Mrs. Owens intimidates her; you can tell by the nervous look in her eye, the quick, flighty movements of her hands, and the way she keeps rocking back and forth in her shoes.

"Mrs. Casey."

She timidly runs her hand through her hair. "Yes?"

"How are the boys doing?"

I look around the office. Pogo Stick and his friends are all lying on cots. They seem to be sluggish but are basically doing well. They're all somewhat bandaged; Pogo has a broken nose and the big kid's arm is in a sling. Frank's sitting in the corner in a chair; I didn't expect to see him here.

"Ah, they seem okay. Nothing broken . . . oh, except for Billy's nose, which I taped tight; there's not much more I can do for it here. I've notified their parents and strongly suggested they all visit the hospital for more thorough examinations."

Mrs. Owens lets out a long sigh and we enter into another one of her prolonged bouts of silence. I can tell she's making everyone, including Mrs. Casey, very anxious and I find myself beginning to admire her interrogation technique. I can see how it would be effective.

She turns to me. "Mr. Saron, do you have something you would like to say to your friends?"

I look over at Frank, and raise my eyebrow slightly. He gives me a quick shake of his head. Does that mean they didn't tell her what happened? It's worth a try. I offer Pogo Stick my best innocent look and say, "What happened to you guys?"

Mrs. Owens snaps, "Oh, please. We all know what's going on here! Mr. Dinatelli informs me that you did this to them."

"Did what to them?"

"You need to just stop this."

I hold up my hands. "Stop what?"

She glares at me. "This innocent routine."

"I don't know what you're talking about."

"I'm talking about how you brutally assaulted these students."

I point at my chest. "You think I did this?" I glance around the room like I'm counting. "You think I beat up seven guys?"

"I think you did and so does Mr. Dinatelli."

I point at my face. "Do I look like I just fought with seven guys? That's almost a baseball team. Look, there's not a scratch on me."

"Mr. Dinatelli said he heard fighting in the locker room. When he went inside to investigate he found these guys on the floor and you walking out the door."

"All that proves is that I walked out of the gym. I could have told you that."

She looks at me, shakes her head, then walks over to Pogo Stick. She softens her voice. The sudden transformation is jarring, like downshifting on the highway. "How are you feeling?"

"Been better."

"I'm sorry to hear that. Do you need anything, Billy?"

"No, I'll be all right."

She smiles, or should I say she tries to smile. You can tell it's not something she's used to doing. "Listen, Billy, I want you to tell me what happened today in the locker room. Okay?"

"Okay."

He looks over at me. We make eye contact. There's something there. It's not fear, guilt, or hate; it's something else. I can't get a read on it.

"Well, it's like this: John and I were standing on the bench seeing who could push who off first, then it kinda turned into which group could push the other group off the bench. Next thing I know, we're all crashing to the hard tile floor together."

Mrs. Owens's head snaps upward. She seems very surprised by his answer. "Are you honestly trying to tell me this was just a simple case of roughhousing?"

"Roughhousing? Is that what you call it? We just call it 'bench wars.'"

Mrs. Owens's lips get really tight. I can see the anger in her eyes. I wonder if Pogo Stick and the other guys can see it too. "So you're telling me that Cody Saron had nothing to do with this, that he didn't beat you boys up?"

"Why would he beat us up? Never mind that, *how* would he beat us up? Like he said, there's seven of us. Is he some kind of superhero?"

Mrs. Owens looks around the room. "Is that right? Are you all telling me you got hurt playing something called *bench wars*?

Everyone nods their heads.

"I don't buy it. Mr. Dinatelli doesn't buy it and anyone who even *glances* at your injuries isn't going to buy it. Now, who's going to step forward and tell me what really happened?"

The room remains quiet. I glance around. Everyone avoids eye contact with me. Mrs. Casey is nervously playing with her stethoscope.

Mrs. Owens lets out a lungful of air. It's like she's been holding her breath. "If that's your story, let me remind you that we don't permit that kind of reckless behavior in our school. Two weeks detention for the lot of you."

I glare at Pogo Stick until I get his attention, then point my chin at Frank, urging him to do the right thing.

"Mrs. Owens, Frank wasn't part of the game. He was just getting dressed. We were playing three against three."

She considers this new information. "Frank."

"Yes, ma'am."

"You should have stepped forward. I think you know what I'm talking about. Three days detention for you."

"But I didn't do anything!"

"Do you want to make it four days?"

"No, ma'am."

She turns and walks out the door. Just like that, she's gone. I thought for sure I was going to be kicked out of school. I didn't even get detention. I can't believe it.

I walk over to Pogo Stick and hold out my hand. At first he just looks at it, then he reaches up and gives it a little slap.

I look over at Mrs. Casey. She's at her desk filling out some paperwork. I lower my voice so she can't hear me. "Thank you."

He smiles. "No problem, but it's gonna cost you."

"What?"

"We want you to teach us how to fight like that."

I nod my head and smile back at him. "No problem."

MATADORS

The wind is whipping around our hair and my ears are cold. We really should have worn hats. We're standing at the edge of a ski trail high in the French Alps. My dad's dressed in his red ski jacket and I have on my thick sweater and black vest. He lifts up his sunglasses; there's that gleam in his eye.

"What do you say, son, want to give it a try?"

The run looks more like the side of a cliff than a trail.

I shout over the wind, "This American guy I met at the ski hut called this run DMD, for Dead Man's Drop."

He raises an eyebrow. "Are you saying you don't want to give it a try?"

"I didn't say that." I glance down the trail again. It's steeper than anything I've ever skied before. "Just saying that I'm . . ."

I don't complete the sentence because my dad suddenly launches himself onto the trail. I watch him expertly plant his pole, swing his body around, and hop; plant his pole, swing his body around, and hop. He keeps planting, swinging, and hopping his way down the side of the steep mountain. He's the matador and the mountain's the bull.

My skis are hanging over the lip of the run. I watch my dad and study his line. If I don't make a mistake, if I don't slip or catch an edge, I can do this. If something goes wrong, I will get hurt. There's no doubt about it: I'll get hurt badly.

I plant my poles, focus on my line, and force myself to remain clear-headed. Once I start, that's it—there's no turning back. My heart is pounding; my muscles twitch in anticipation. I take a deep breath, drive all the negative thoughts away, and push off.

Crack.

My eyes spring open wide. I grab the knife from under my pillow. What was that sound?

I'm lying in bed. I glance over at the digital clock. It's glowing 2:35.

I heard something; I know I did. For five days now, I've been able to sleep without doing my little nightly recon missions through the woods. I've managed to convince myself that I was being overly cautious and maybe just plain paranoid. But this is different, this is real, there definitely was a sound outside.

I slip out of my bed, quickly dress in the dark, and grab the small leather bag I've hidden in the closet. It contains my stash of homemade weapons: eight sharp metal spikes with tail feathers, a powerful slingshot, and nunchucks. My dad would be proud. I assembled everything exactly like he taught me, using stuff I found in the garage.

There's a window in the laundry room that's covered outside by a large, thick bush. A while ago I trimmed away some of the branches close to the house so I could slither through it and crawl unnoticed into the woods.

It's been less than six minutes since I heard the sound and now I'm wide awake and moving silently from tree to tree. It's a pitch-black, new-moon night and I know I'm not alone. There's something wrong, a little too much noise for just the wind. I move in the quiet catlike manner my dad taught me.

I'm scared and I exhale the fear, then try to slurp it up like soup. Fear can be like fuel, it can keep you moving and focused. I feel more alive than I have in weeks. I've stepped out of the domestic world and back into the wild. I understand the rules here; they're simple and easy to follow. You're either the hunter or the prey.

The air is crisp and cool; my breath fogs slightly as it leaves my mouth, everything is damp with dew.

I sense that I'm missing something. It's a tugging sensation, like a forgotten anchor left dragging under the boat. My dad always told me to trust my gut. He said it can pick up information that your brain's taken in but hasn't been able to digest yet.

I take off my belt and use it to quietly haul myself up a tree, into that safe envelope of space between the earth and the dark sky. I wrap my arms and legs around a large, thick branch and disappear. I need a moment to try to piece together what's going on.

Just a few hours ago I was safe and warm with Jenny, watching an old tape of her and my mother playing soccer when they were kids. Now here I am in the woods, hanging from a tree.

I let the minutes pass. My eyes adjust to the darkness. I decide that I'm comfortable enough. I'll wait here and let whoever's out there come to me. I study the darkness, looking for shapes or changes, listening to every sound.

I struggle to see what I feel.

The problem with this kind of heightened awareness is that after a while you start to see shapes and movement where there isn't any. There's a shadow that looks like it's moving in my direction. It has to be my imagination because it's moving way too fast. If a person was moving that fast they'd be making a ton of noise.

I slowly remove my slingshot and load it with one of the spikes. I aim it at the quickly approaching shadow; still reluctant to believe it's a person. I start to breathe harder. It's moving too fast, noiselessly heading toward me like it's walking on air.

It's within striking distance of my spike. It's definitely a person; I can make out the arms, the legs, and the chest. He's a large, bulky man dressed completely in black, wearing a ski mask and carrying a high-powered rifle with a scope. I pull back the sling-shot even farther and keep it aimed at his chest.

He stops, crouches down to the ground, and creeps over to the tree line. His hands are moving back and forth, searching through the dirt and leaves. After a few minutes he reaches under a bush and finds something. It looks like a small metal box. He slips it into his pocket and inches his way back into the thicker woods.

He stands and starts moving again, still heading in my direction. How does he move so quickly without making a sound? I know I'm securely hidden up here but there's still that element of doubt and fear. What if I'm not as invisible as I think I am?

Can he hear my breathing, the pounding of my heart? He's almost directly below me.

Snap.

He doesn't move, just freezes, then he squats down low and readies his rifle. I heard it too, that noise, the breaking of a branch or a twig, maybe forty feet away in the thick underbrush.

The man in black sweeps the woods behind us with what appears to be a SIG 550 assault rifle, looking through its large scope. Is it a night-vision scope? I can't tell, but I think so. There's definitely a silencer screwed onto the end of the barrel, which I wasn't sure you could do. It certainly is a very nasty weapon. I wish I had one.

My arm is starting to get tired from holding back the spike in the slingshot. It's starting to shake and my fingers are cramping. I will away the pain and keep focused on my target.

Just when I'm at the point where I don't think I can hold back the slingshot any longer, the man in black stands and starts to quickly move again in that silent manner of his. He glides effortlessly away; I watch his dark form until it's soaked up into the shadows of the night.

I ease off the slingshot and rest my whole body against the thick branch. My arm feels like it's burning, my fingers are numb and I'm covered in sweat.

Who was that guy? And what is he doing out here? Is he going to the cottage? Is Jenny in danger?

I get the feeling that if he wanted to get into our cottage he would have been there by now. He moves too smoothly, too professionally; it would take a small army to stop him from his objective. If it was the cottage, he would have struck hard and fast.

I sense movement again but not from the direction the man in black disappeared into. I turn and look toward the place where I first saw him. I study the surrounding darkness, looking for shapes and patterns. Yes, it looks like there's someone there but he's not moving as quickly as the last man. He's quiet, moves well, but he doesn't glide.

My arm is still tired but fear has given me a renewed sense of strength. I reload the spike and pull back on the slingshot's cord. I study the advancing form. Maybe I've underestimated him. He's also moving very quietly, but unlike the man in black he's advancing using trees and rocks as continuous cover. I never really have a clear target.

Something about the way the form moves seems familiar. I struggle to get a good look at him. When he shifts between a rock and a bush close to me I spot the missing arm. It's Andy.

I ease off the slingshot. I notice he's carrying a pistol, a nice nine-millimeter Glock. I'll have to ask him to show it to me later. Unfortunately, any thought I had of letting him know I'm here vanishes with that discovery. If I try to tip him off to my location there's a really good chance I could be mistakenly shot.

Andy's close to my tree; he stops and squats down where the man in black had stopped. He's examining the dirt; I think he spotted something. Good job, Andy.

He moves over to my tree, leans against the trunk. If I wanted to, I could hang down and tap him on the shoulder. I imagine that would really freak him out. It would almost be worth the risk of getting shot, just to see his reaction.

He continues onward, over to another tree, then a bush, then behind and over a rock before being swallowed by the darkness.

I lie across my branch wondering if I should return to the ground and try to track the two men. I feel worn out and tired, my shirt's soaked through with sweat. I squint at my watch. An hour—that should do it. I tell myself not to move for one hour. I'm not the matador my dad is.

THE SILENT SUIT

"Cody?"

"Yeah, Dad?"

"It's time for IDs."

He hands me a passport. I open it up and glance at the picture.

"Who am I this time?"

Beep, beep, beep . . .

I swim up from the depths of sleep, grasping for the alarm clock. My hand fumbles around the night table like a blind spider.

How come I can't find something so loud and so close?

I brush against it and almost knock it to the floor. I grab the clock as it hangs over the table by its cord.

My hands feel disconnected from my body and my eyes just don't want to open. I struggle to find the little switch to turn off the alarm. I know it's red but that only helps if you have your eyes open. Finally I find it and the alarm falls silent. I've conquered the alarm clock. There should be a special reward for this grand accomplishment, like maybe eight more hours of sleep.

My feet swing out of bed and onto the floor.

Other kids live normal lives, other kids spend all their time figuring out what to wear and how to act, but no, not me. I've gotta run around in the woods all night chasing people with assault rifles. I've gotta have cafés blow up around me. I've gotta hide in some small town like a fugitive.

I shuffle into the bathroom and look in the mirror. I'm covered in dirt and my arms and chest are all scratched up from hanging onto that stupid branch all night. Great, just great.

I take the world's longest shower. Warm water cascades down my body. I feel like I could stay here all day. It's also another excuse to keep my eyes closed.

Two lousy hours, that's all the sleep I got last night. Oh, I guess you could add the couple hours before I woke up, but still it's not enough.

What a crazy night. . . . Who was that guy? And what was he doing in the woods? And what was that little metal box? Should I tell Jenny about it? I'm not sure. Maybe I should talk to Andy first. I'm betting Jenny would call the police right away and I don't think that would be a good thing. They'd ask a whole lot of questions, it's their nature.

Knock. Knock. Knock.

"Cody? Are you okay in there?"

I yell over the water. "Yeah. Be out in a sec."

"Better hurry. You're going to be late."

I dry off and head back to my room. I grab one of the outfits Albert picked out for me and quickly get changed. Wide pants and a huge white T-shirt with some guy's name written across the front.

There's a mirror behind my door. I stand in front of it and study my reflection. I feel like I'm playing a part in a movie. This just isn't me. Who is this guy? I know this is what everyone else wears but I can't get used to it. I've tried, I really have, and now I'm just too tired to care.

I open the closet and look at my suit.

Jenny's cup of coffee stops midway between the kitchen table and her mouth. "Wow, Cody. That's . . . what are you wearing?"

I look at my sleeves and adjust my tie. "Haven't you ever seen a suit before?"

"Well, yeah, of course, but why are you wearing one today? Is there a class picture or something?"

"No, I just feel more comfortable wearing suits. It's what I'm used to. I'm sick of trying to be someone I'm not. This is the real me."

"Okay . . . but aren't you worried the kids will give you a hard time?"

"Oh, I don't care anymore. I don't have time to figure out this whole *clothes* thing. A guy could spend hours just trying to pick out the right T-shirt." I hold out my arms for her inspection. "Besides, it's an Armani."

"You're going to wear an Armani to school? Aren't you worried something will happen to it?"

"I've worn suits to worse places than a junior high school."

I walk over to the stove. "Could I have some of these scrambled eggs?"

"Cody, I made them for both of us. Every morning I make you breakfast and every morning you ask if it's okay for you to take some. You don't have to ask. Just take, okay?"

She seems hurt. I'm not sure why. It wouldn't be polite to take something without asking first.

I pile some eggs onto my plate, grab a glass of orange juice, and sit next to her. I glare at the clock above the sink: You too? All the clocks in the house are conspiring against me today. I can't possibly be this late. I was hoping to catch Andy before heading to the bus stop. I shovel eggs into my mouth and gulp down orange juice.

Jenny's not eating. She's just staring at me over her cup of coffee. I can feel her eyes burning into the side of my head.

I turn to her. "What?"

"I know you're running late, but you look like you've entered a scrambled egg eating contest."

"Sorry."

"No need to be sorry. Just slow down a bit."

"Okay."

"You know, it wouldn't kill you to talk to me in the mornings."

I look up from my eggs. "I guess I'm not a big talker."

"You were able to talk to me the other night. I think it helped both of us."

Just the memory of telling her about the café brings it all rushing back. I can hear my dad yelling, "Go! Go! Go!" I put my fork down. I'm not hungry anymore.

My eyes itch. I rub them longer than I have to. I'm so tired. I don't have the strength for one of these chitchat sinkholes. Couldn't we have this conversation tomorrow?

She smiles one of those far-away smiles. "Remember when you were four and I caught up with you guys in Mexico City? You sure could talk up a storm back then."

"Kind of, but not really."

"You were so cute. You had this little puppet that you'd make me talk to. He was a hand puppet with a big sombrero. What was his name again? You used to call him . . . oh, I just can't remember."

"Mr. Pedro."

She chuckles. "Yes! That's it. Mr. Pedro! He was so adorable. Whatever happened to Mr. Pedro?"

I think about it for a moment. "Um, Dad put him in the exhaust pipe of some guy's car."

"Why did he do that?"

"He told me that Mr. Pedro had a new and very important job, making sure the bad man with the black hat didn't go anywhere."

She looks at me for a moment, blinking her eyes like she's having trouble taking in this information. "Seriously? That's what happened to Mr. Pedro?"

"Yup. Mr. Pedro made the ultimate sacrifice. He gave up his life in the service of our country."

Her face changes; sadness sweeps over it. I thought it was a funny joke.

"What's the matter? Did I say something wrong?"

"That's what the letter from the president said about my sister Jodi." She looks up at me. "Your mother."

"Really?"

"Yeah, but it didn't make me feel any better. I don't think any letter could have done that."

I'm surprised to see a tear slip down her cheek. Can pain really last that long? I thought time heals everything.

I try to think of some comforting words to say but I have too many questions of my own. I know I shouldn't ask, but I can't help myself. The words slip out of my mouth. "Do you still have the letter?"

She shakes her head. "No. I wish I did, but I ripped it up into tiny pieces."

We sit together in this snakelike silence. I briefly consider asking her more questions about my mother. I love when we talk about my mother but maybe it would be best if I just change the subject, keep things light for now.

I blurt out, "Maybe you're right. I really should try to talk more. Why don't we talk about something fun. What would you like to talk about?"

She lets out a long breath of air; she seems relieved that I changed the subject. "Oh, Cody, it doesn't matter. Anything. What do other people talk about?"

I'm not like "other people"—doesn't she know that by now? "Other people" don't spend their nights chasing mystery men around in the woods. "Other people" don't toss six kids around a locker room like they were paper airplanes. "Other people" don't spend their spare time making lethal weapons out of slingshots and steel spikes.

My shoulders shrug all by themselves. "Um, I don't know. I guess they talk about television."

"I'm sure they talk about more than just television. Maybe they talk about their days or what they'd like to do on the weekend. You know, that kind of stuff."

"Sounds about right."

She studies me for what seems like a full minute. "Cody . . . I swear, sometimes you drive me crazy. It's like living with a robot."

"What do you mean?"

"Sometimes you go hours without talking. Why is it so difficult for you? What ever happened to that little boy?"

My eyebrows move up my forehead. "I've been talking ever since I walked into the kitchen."

"You answer questions. That's not the same as talking."

"I asked if I could have some eggs."

She shakes her head. "Nope, that's not the same thing."

"Sure it is."

"No, it's not. Listen, I'm not trying to be a pain. I just want us to talk more. That's all. Can we do that? I mean *really* try to do that?"

My dad and I would sometimes go days without talking. It never really bothered me much. That's just the way it was. It never occurred to me that being quiet could disturb someone.

I force a smile. "Sure, we can do that."

"Thanks. So . . . let's see . . ." She struggles to collect her thoughts. "I want you to feel free to talk to me about anything, and I mean *anything* . . . do you know what I mean?"

I think about the mystery man in the woods, his assault rifle, and the little metal box. Then there's the café bombing, the fact that someone's trying to kill my dad, and the added stress of being forced to lead a life I've never lived before.

"Um, I guess . . . well, kind of."

She leans forward, and even though we're all alone she lowers her voice. "You know . . . you could also talk about *girls*, and the way guys your age start to feel about them, that kind of thing."

My head snaps up. That wasn't what I expected her to say. I thought she'd want to talk about books or maybe the weather. I avoid eye contact. "Um, thanks, Jenny. I'll keep that in mind."

"Don't be embarrassed. Seriously, you can talk to me anytime. Okay?"

"Okay."

She flashes me a smile. "So . . . do you have a girlfriend?"

I stare at my eggs. I can feel my cheeks reddening. "No."

"Really? Good-looking guy like you doesn't have a girlfriend? I thought maybe that's why you're wearing your suit today. Nothing wrong with trying to impress a girl."

"No, really. I just feel more comfortable in suits. I've always worn a suit. Me and my dad."

She reaches over and flicks a piece of lint off my sleeve. "Well, you wear a suit well. You look very handsome. Your dad used to wear suits when we were just teenagers. He had this part-time job at a local men's clothing store. But I think you might wear a suit even better than he did."

"Really?"

"Definitely. He lived right next door to us so I saw him all the time. You look more natural than he did. He used to *swagger*. He'd come home from work, park his car, and then *swagger* over to our house and try to impress us. I think Jodi fell for his dress-up routine but I've always liked a guy who acts natural."

"Girls like guys who act natural?"

"Sure do. Is there a girl you're interested in?"

Even though the conversation is shifting it's still making me very uncomfortable. I glance at the clock. Time's slipping away. I really want to talk to Andy before school but for some reason the word "Maybe" escapes from my lips.

She seems excited. "Really? What's her name?"

How did I travel down this road? I've got to get some sleep. I sit and blink at her, not really sure if I want to reveal my secret. "What?"

"The girl's name. What's her name?"

"Um . . . Renee Carrington. She's in my history class. We're working on a project together about France during the American Revolution."

"That sounds fantastic. Working together on a project can be a great way to get to know each other better." She stops talking; she has this look on her face like she just remembered something. "There's something about her name. Why does it sound so familiar? Renee Carrington? Is that Annie Carrington's little sister?"

I'm confused. "Who's Annie Carrington?"

"You know. She's Andy's friend. I saw you talking to her in the driveway. She drives that car with the big engine."

"That's Renee's sister?"

"I don't know. That's what I'm asking you. Annie Carrington

was in my yoga class. I know she has a much younger sister who she takes care of, but I don't know if her name's Renee."

I pick up my fork and shovel some eggs into my mouth while I think about this new information. I mumble through a mouthful of food, "I guess it could be. I'll have to ask Andy."

Jenny cocks her head to the side and her eyebrows rise slightly. "Is she cute?"

I think about the question. "Yeah, that's a good word for her, cute."

"Are you comfortable talking to her?"

"Yeah, I guess . . . a little. You know."

"Well, don't forget to listen, too."

"Okay."

"No, really, if you want a girl to like you, listen to her. Get her to open up about herself."

"Okay."

She puts her hand on my shoulder. "Seriously, anytime you want to talk to me about girls, feel free. I've got inside information that I'm willing to part with."

I'm not sure why, but hearing that makes me feel really good. I understand stuff like disarming bombs, alarm systems, and guys with guns, but when it comes to girls I could use a little help.

I smile and mutter, "Thanks."

"So, we'll talk?"

"I'd like that."

"About everything, the good and the bad?"

I nod my head. "Yeah, everything."

She reaches out and roughs up my hair. For some reason it doesn't bother me. I kinda like it. I wonder if that's something my mom would have done too.

I glance at the clock. "No! These clocks, I swear." I bolt to my feet. "I'm really late. I've gotta run."

I gently tap on Andy's bedroom window.

The curtains move just the slightest bit, as if someone's peeking around the corner and then they're yanked to the side and he's standing there in his underwear. He looks wide awake although I'm sure he was sleeping just five seconds ago.

With his shirt off he seems more muscular, almost square, like one of those Rock 'em Sock 'em Robots my dad and I used to play with. He's also got a nice tattoo on his shoulder; it's a cobra with a knife in its mouth. I avoid looking at the stump of his missing arm and the long scar across his side.

He opens the window and grins. "What's up with the suit?"

"I'm sick of wearing clothes I don't understand."

He gives me a puzzled look. "Okay, that doesn't make a whole lot of sense to me right now, but then again I just woke up."

I cover my mouth; it's something my dad taught me, an added precaution in case someone's watching you. "We've got to talk."

His grin turns into a smile. "Well, I don't know a whole lot about suits but you look all right to me."

I keep my hand over my mouth. "No, we've got to talk about last night."

The smile disappears. "What about last night?"

"I saw you in the woods."

"Really?"

"Yeah, and I saw the man you were tracking."

His face changes; he becomes very serious. He pushes the window open wider, leans forward, and lowers his voice. "Really? You saw the ghost?"

"The ghost?"

"That's what I call him because I've never seen him and he's so quiet. I was beginning to wonder if I was just being paranoid. I thought maybe all these flashbacks of the war were starting to mess with my mind."

I remember the way he moved. "The ghost" is an excellent name. "No, you're not being paranoid. I heard something last night and I went to investigate—"

Andy interrupts me. "That was my trap, he sprung my trap. I couldn't believe it. He's avoided all my others and trips a simple log-drop. Afterward I was beginning to wonder if it was just a deer."

"No, it wasn't a deer, that's for sure. I saw him. I was perched in a tree. Big guy, dressed in black, ski mask, moved fast and completely silent. Professional. Dangerous. Had a nasty weapon, you should be glad you didn't catch up with him."

"Armed with what?"

I struggle to remember the name of the weapon, I almost give up, then it comes to me. "A SIG 550 assault rifle with what looked like a night scope."

"Seriously?"

I nod my head. "Yeah."

"Oh man, what's going on here?"

"I was hoping you'd have some ideas."

He shakes his head. "It's a mystery to me. What was he doing? Did you see anything?"

"Yeah, he got some kind of metal box that was hidden by the tree line."

Andy's eyes open a little wider. "Huh? By the tree line? How big was it?"

"About this big." I show him with my hands. "What do you think it was?"

He clenches his jaw tightly. His expression looks grim. "We can't talk about this now. Not here. We'll discuss it later. I feel like I'm wading into something without knowing how deep it is. I think it's time I know a little more about your past."

"About my past?"

"Now's not the time. We'll talk later."

"But—"

He holds up his hand. "I said later."

"Okay." I start to walk away then stop. "Andy?"

"Later."

"It's about something else."

"What?"

I look at my polished shoes. "Um, your friend Annie, is her last name Carrington?"

"It is."

"Does she have a sister, Renee?"

"She does. Why?"

"Um, she's in my history class. I better run. Talk to you later."

I start to walk away.

"Cody."

I turn around. "Yeah."

"Keep your eyes open. Be careful."

That's what my dad had told me. I nod my head and walk toward the bus stop.

THE RUNNING
OF THE MICE

I thought I was going to miss the bus, but the usual collection of kids are still standing at the stop, side by side like books on a shelf.

Why do they do that? You'd think they'd walk around or something, but they just stand there staring across the street into the woods. It's kind of eerie, almost like they're prisoners awaiting execution. They might as well tie blindfolds around their heads.

I join the group fully expecting everyone to take one look at my suit and then rip me apart like a fortune cookie, but nobody says anything, not one word, not even "Good morning."

I study Albert. He's messing with his backpack. Like he

suddenly has to find something in there that's really important. He seems angry.

"Hey . . . is everything all right?"

He digs deeper in his backpack and doesn't look at me. "Yeah, everything's fine. Just looking for something."

"What are you looking for?"

"Ah, you know, um, stuff . . . stuff that I . . . can't seem to find."

He continues to dig. Unless he's got something sewed into the lining of his pack, I don't think he's going to find whatever he's looking for.

"You sure everything's all right?"

"Yeah, fine." His voice sounds different.

Something's wrong. I'm used to people giving me a hard time, it's what they do. I stare at Albert, sifting through his books like he's panning for gold. I'm getting aggravated. I should tie him to a tree and force him to make fun of my suit.

I glance at Cell Phone Girl. She quickly looks away. The redheaded iPod girl has her back to me; her music is blasting, she's safely enclosed in her little bubble of noise. There are two other kids I've never talked to before. I've always thought of them as Neighborhood Kid A and Neighborhood Kid B. Both of them are standing at attention, staring straight ahead, like those unblinking English guards assigned to protect the queen.

Albert just keeps on digging but I think if he could, he'd leave his books by the side of the road and crawl into that pack. What's going on here?

Cell Phone Girl's phone goes off with some hip-hop ringtone I've never heard before. Instead of answering it, she just lets it ring and looks at me. There's a pleading, apologetic look in her eyes, the same kind of look you'd give someone if you accidentally ran over their cat in the driveway.

"Aren't you going to answer that?"

She digs the phone out of her bag.

"Hello . . . Yeah, um, I can't talk right now. . . . I'll call you later. . . . No, really I can't. . . . Seriously, I can't. . . . You know why. . . . Yes . . . *Yes* . . . I gotta go. Bye. . . . I will. Bye . . . Bye."

She clicks the phone shut, slips it back into her bag, and desperately tries to act natural, standing there, looking around, doing everything but whistle. I feel like we're all playing tennis with a bowling ball.

Albert zips up his pack. I walk over to him. "What's going on?"

He shakes his head and mutters, "You know."

"Know what? I don't know anything."

He glares at me, points at the others, and snaps, "They all think you're some kind of crazy psychopath." Then pointing at himself, "And I'm mad that you broke the code!"

"What code? What are you talking about?"

"I haven't told Andy yet but I'm sure he's going to be upset, too."

I throw up my arms. "What code? I have no idea what you're talking about!"

"My sensei at the dojo taught us that the first rule of karate is to hide your karate like a buried treasure. That means you don't go around busting heads just because you can. You only use it to defend yourself."

"I *was* defending myself, and Frank Flynn, too. They were pushing us around in the gym. Someone kicked me in the back. Pogo Stick threw a punch at me. Hey, it was six against one."

Albert rolls his eyes, shakes his head, and growls, "You're such a . . ." He stops and gains control of his anger. "That's not the story I heard. Everyone said you just went crazy and almost killed those guys. They think you're a seriously messed-up psycho. And I think they might be right."

I hold up my hands. "That's not what happened. Really. Why would I do that? It doesn't make any sense. Besides, how does *everyone* even know about it? All this just happened yesterday."

"What planet are you from? This is all everybody's talking about. You know, cell phones, e-mails, someone even posted a video on YouTube. They reenacted the whole episode using G.I. Joe dolls."

"Really?" I can't believe this.

"Hey, you're a star. You're the talk of the school. I guess that's why you're wearing the suit. Getting ready for your big close-up, Mr. Hollywood?"

"I'm wearing the suit because I like wearing suits, that's all."

"Yeah, right, whatever you say."

This is another fine example of why this whole school routine can just drive a guy completely nuts. I didn't have to deal with this kind of stuff when it was just me and my dad. Maybe that's the real purpose of school: to drive everyone bonkers.

I wonder if it's even worth trying to convince him what really happened. He seems to have made up his mind based on what he's heard and some stupid homemade video using dolls. It surprises me how much his anger hurts.

I guess I value his friendship more than I realized.

The bus finally bounces around the corner, giving me an excuse to put off this conversation until I can figure out what to say.

For once the sight of the Yankees-capped, unsmiling bus driver who wears a road map for a face is a welcome one. She swings open the door and the others wait for me to enter. As I walk up the stairs, the noise level of the bus dims with each step I take.

I stand at the head of the aisle looking for an open seat. Everyone seems to be staring at me and I don't think it's because of my clothes.

A guy in the fourth row yells, "Ready . . . aim . . . suit!"

He laughs at his own joke until a girl behind him leans forward and whispers into his ear. The smile on his face is instantly replaced with alarm.

Someone I've never seen before in the back of the bus stands and shouts, "Hey, Cody! Back here, I saved you a seat!"

I'm more curious than anything else. I see a few other empty seats, but who is this big kid with the black leather jacket and multiple facial piercings? Why is he so desperate for me to sit with him?

There are two really good-looking girls sitting in the seat next to him, waving. "Yeah, Cody! Sit with us!"

I walk to the back of the bus. The guy with the leather jacket extends his hand. I go to shake it but he starts with some kind of bizarre handshake I don't understand, grabbing, punching, and pointing. My dad told me that a handshake is the measure of a man. This is more like synchronized swimming; I'm not sure what it's supposed to measure.

In the end we revert to the conventional handshake I'm familiar with.

"Cody, good to see you again. I'd like to introduce you to the girls. This here is Amber, and that's Nicki."

Both girls smile and call out together, "Hey, Cody."

He grabs my arm. "Come on, sit down, sit down."

I'm pulled down next to him and he moves in close. The smell of leather, cigarettes, and his foul breath is overpowering. He speaks in a dull, steady voice like some kind of cave-dwelling creature. "The girls, they really wanted to meet you. I told them not to worry, I'd introduce you. I always keep my word."

"Do I know you?"

He laughs—it sounds like nuts and bolts being shaken in a can—and gives me a light punch on the shoulder. "Duh, I'm in your Spanish class."

"You are?"

"Yeah, of course, I sit in the back row by the door. Actually, I haven't been to class in a while but I was there for your first day. You know, when you got kicked out."

I study his face; he looks like he could be sixteen. Did he stay back a few times? I think I've seen him around school but I'm not sure. "I'm sorry. I don't remember your name."

"It's Troy, Troy Sampson. Everybody knows who I am. Ask around." He lowers his voice. "If you ever want anything, I mean anything at all, I'm your man."

I stare at the back of the seat in front of me trying to figure out what "anything" in a junior high school could mean. I've come across guys like Troy all over the world. Every town and city has a Troy. Sometimes they can be useful, but more often than not they're magnets for trouble who should be avoided.

"I'll keep that in mind."

He smiles. "Do that. I don't disappoint. Now how about meeting the girls?"

"Um, sure."

He puts his arm around my shoulder and gives me a little shake. "Oh, one more thing. I really like this suit. I mean it's totally you, totally cool. What a great statement. It's very . . . *American Gangster*. I loved that movie."

"Thanks . . . um, I guess."

Troy winks, then switches seats with the girls. They squeeze in next to me. Both of them talk really fast. They're very attractive but equally annoying; it's like mixing sugar and salt. All things considered, I think I'd rather be left alone. Besides, all they really want to talk about is the fight. I don't want to talk about it.

The ride takes forever. I really hate this bus.

School, with its mirrored front doors and kids scurrying around like very loud, backpack-clad cockroaches, is a welcome sight. I'm not sure how much longer I could have lasted with Amber and Nicki. How could a conversation with two beautiful girls prove to be so mind-numbingly painful? I seriously considered launching myself out that emergency exit door on a number of occasions.

Troy and the girls walk with me to the school. I try to act like we all just happen to be walking in the same direction but they keep talking to me, asking questions and laughing like we're sharing the world's biggest joke together.

When we march into school the first person I see is Frank Flynn. He's leaning against a wall. His huge bulk makes him look like he's sinking into it.

We make eye contact and he quickly signals me to join him. I nod back my agreement.

I turn to Troy. "Hey, I've got to talk to someone. See you later."

He seems both surprised and disappointed. "Um, sure. No problem. I'm always around. Remember what I said about if you ever need anything."

"Yeah, um, I'll remember."

His fist is between us. Hovering in the air, waiting for me to start the mystical handshake of the self-proclaimed cool kids. I've had enough. I briefly consider a quick roundhouse to his chin instead but dismiss the idea, although it's not without merit.

I grab his fist and pump it up and down a few times before dismissing him. If he senses my annoyance, he doesn't let on.

Amber and Nicki smile, give me little girl waves and a sing-song, "Bye-bye, Cody!"

Nicki blows me a kiss before the two girls link arms and glide down the hall together. They seem magnetic—all the guys turn and watch them walk by.

I've been wondering what my mother was like when she was my age. I'm sure she wasn't like that. Maybe she was quiet and kept to herself. I really don't know. I'll have to ask Jenny.

I walk over to Frank. "What's up?"

"What are you doing with Troy Sampson?"

"You know him?"

He shakes his head in disgust. "I don't know him. I just know *of* him. Everyone does. Troy is trouble. Last year he shoved my head in a toilet. I think he's shoved everyone's head in a toilet. He's not someone you want to be friends with."

"He's not my friend."

"That's not what it looked like to me. You guys seemed real chummy."

I can feel a smile tugging its way onto my face. "Did you say *chummy*?"

He stops leaning on the wall and stands up straight. "Well, you know what I mean, you looked friendly. Listen, all I'm saying is watch out, he's the Tony Soprano of our school."

"Who's Tony Soprano?"

"You know, of *The Sopranos*."

"What are the sopranos?"

His eyes open wide. "Haven't you ever heard of the show, *The Sopranos*?"

"Sorry, I don't watch television."

"Well, that's just . . . well, it's just weird. Who doesn't watch TV?"

"I guess I don't."

"Well, the point is, watch out for Troy, he's trouble."

I pat him on the shoulder. "Don't worry, Frank. I don't like the guy. I don't even like his two girlfriends."

"You mean Amber and Nicki?"

"Yeah."

Frank looks up and down the hall before covering his mouth

and leaning forward. His voice is so low I can barely hear it. "Rumor has it they'll do absolutely *anything* he tells them to do."

"I guess that's . . . interesting to know."

Frank starts to laugh. His whole body shakes. "That's one way to put it, 'interesting to know.'"

He stops laughing and gets serious. "Cody, I have to tell you something."

"Sure, what's the matter?"

His gaze falls to the floor. "It's about yesterday."

"What about it?"

"Um, I just wanted to apologize."

"Hey, you didn't do anything wrong. It was the other guys who were being jerks."

He stops looking at the floor and looks me in the eye. "Yeah, they were jerks but I should have done something to help. I'm sorry."

"Hey, don't worry about it."

"It's just that the whole thing kinda freaked me out. I've never seen anything like that before. It all happened so fast. I thought they were all . . . well, you know what I thought."

"Like I said, don't worry about it. Okay?"

"Okay . . . Thanks."

He steps backward and gives me an appraising look. "So, now that I got that out of the way, tell me something—what's up with the suit?"

"Nothing. I just feel more comfortable in suits."

"Yeah, well, I feel more comfortable in my pajamas and slippers but you don't see me wearing them to school."

I start to laugh, picturing Frank walking around the halls in his pajamas. "I grew up with my dad. I've always worn a suit. When I dress like I've been dressing here in school, to me it feels like I'm wearing my pajamas in public."

"What did you wear at your other schools?"

I've got to be more careful. This is why it doesn't pay to talk about yourself. After a while you slip out from under the cover you've created. You start slowly revealing more and more about the real you. My dad used to say, "Don't talk; walk." It meant don't get close to anyone.

I clear my throat. "Um, at my other schools we always had to wear uniforms."

"Uniforms. Oh, man, I'd really hate that, but a uniform's not the same as a suit."

I smile. "It's practically the same."

"I guess. Hey, you wanna head up to the science labs? I know these two guys; they're going to let all the lab mice run free in the halls before school starts. I have this crazy idea that it's going to be like the running of the bulls, only with mice. It could be fun to watch."

I think about the possibilities. I don't have to think very long. "Sounds great. Let's go."

The walk through the now-familiar halls is completely different than any other day at school. Suddenly everyone seems to know who I am. In a way I *have* become "Mr. Hollywood." As we move along, elbows are being jabbed into the sides of friends, chins are being raised in my direction, conversations stop, and whispering begins.

Some people like this kind of attention. I don't. Neither would my dad. I'm sure he'd be disappointed. When we said good-bye at the airport he gave me a big hug and said, "Remember, don't do anything to draw attention to yourself, just blend in. Become the invisible boy."

Frank and I pass by the large mirror that asks ARE YOU LOOKING AT AN HONOR STUDENT? I admire the cut of my suit, the silk tie, the polished Italian shoes. Honor student? Hardly, but a vast improvement over the girls' gym uniform I was recently forced to wear.

I run right into Renee. When I say run into, I don't mean I see her in the hall. I mean I'm too busy admiring myself in the mirror to watch where I'm going.

Her books crash to the floor and she makes a strange yipping sound, like when you accidentally step on a dog's tail. We both reach down to pick up the books at the same time and we really slam our heads together. Renee holds her head and leans against a row of lockers. Her eyes fill with tears.

I quickly move to her side. I understand how she feels. I'm

feeling out of it myself. There are little black spots distorting my vision, dancing in front of my eyes like a swarm of gnats. I feel like I'm moving in slow motion. The last time I felt like this was when I was learning how to use a pair of nunchucks and I accidentally slammed one against my forehead. I had a huge knot on my head for two weeks.

"Renee, Renee, I'm sorry, are you okay?"

She's shaking her head and blinking her eyes. "That *really* hurt!"

"I know. I guess we both have hard heads."

She stares at me for a while. I can see the focus slowly coming back into her eyes. In a low voice she says, "You know something?"

I lean forward. "What?"

"You're such an idiot."

I feel like buildings are crashing down inside my chest. I try my best to smile but it's really hard. "If it's any consolation, I feel like an idiot."

There's a small crowd gathering around us. I hear someone ask, "What happened?" Then the clear, loud reply: "That guy Cody just beat up some girl."

I turn in their direction and hold up my hands. "No, no . . . that's not what happened, really. I didn't hit her. I swear. It was a mistake, an accident. We hit our heads together picking up her books."

The crowd looks skeptical. Then a voice in the back says, "He's lying. I saw the whole thing. He just went crazy and threw her against the lockers."

"No, I didn't, really! It was an accident."

I move toward the crowd to plead my case and they quickly back away from me. I can see that they don't believe me. I also see the fear and mistrust in their eyes. I've become some kind of horrible monster, like Frankenstein's creature.

I give up and move back to Renee's side. "How's the head? You okay?"

She seems more irritated than hurt. "What's wrong with you? I mean it. I heard about your fight yesterday. Do you *like* hurting people? Did you enjoy hurting me?"

"No, of course not! I said I was sorry. I really meant it. It was an accident. You must know that."

She gives me an icy glare. "I'm a vegetarian. I bet you didn't know that."

"What's that got to do with anything?"

"I'm not surprised you don't get it. I don't eat meat because I think it's cruel. What makes you think I'd want to be seen with someone who goes around hurting people for the fun of it?"

"I don't hurt people for the fun—"

She holds up her hand. "Cody, I don't want to hear it! Don't talk to me. Where are my books? I just want to get out of here before you kick me in the head or something."

"Please, Renee, don't be like this. . . . Um, what about France?"

"Forget France . . . just give me my books."

Frank hands her the books and she takes off down the hall, her heels angrily tapping away on the tile floor. I watch her walk and wonder the whole time if I should try to stop her or just let her go.

When she rounds the corner Frank says, "You should have stopped her."

"You really think so?"

He starts to laugh. "No way. Are you crazy? She would have killed you. I don't know anything about girls, but I know when someone's mad. And she was *really* mad. I think you should give her some time to cool down."

"I guess . . . maybe you're right."

He gives me a long, appraising look. "Oh, I get it. You like her, don't you?"

I can feel my cheeks reddening. Why do they keep doing that? "Well, I guess, maybe, kind of."

He keeps looking at me and nods his head. I'm embarrassed that I parted with this information. He doesn't seem to know what to do with it. We stand together in silence. I glance again at the mirror. I somehow look smaller, even with my suit.

Frank points his chin down the hallway. "Um, you wanna see if we can still catch the running of the mice?"

URBAN LEGEND

In the end the mice never ran free. The science lab hall filled with students, not mice. It seems like everyone in the school heard the rumor and came upstairs hoping to catch the rodent rampage.

I've noticed there's always one crazy rumor or another floating around this school. If half the things happened that were rumored to happen, this would be one of the oddest places on earth. I can only imagine what they're saying about me.

I should have known nothing was going to happen with the mice. Freeing them would have involved picking a lock or stealing a key. I doubt anyone around here is capable of performing such a simplistic feat.

When the crowd grows restless I briefly consider just doing it myself but decide it's not worth the risk. I've become the center of attention. It would be tough to sneak around picking locks with everyone staring at me.

The school will just have to find some comfort in the fact that I'm the grand consolation prize. If it's not going to be overrun by rodents at least it's got me, Cody the Psychopath, to hold its attention.

I plow through the remainder of the morning feeling like a large poisonous snake. Everybody flashes me the same nervous smile and flinches if I move my hands too quickly. When I walk down the crowded halls they part in front of me. Laughter stops when I get close to it. Classrooms grow quiet when I pass into them.

Even teachers treat me differently. They stand as far away from me as possible, avoid eye contact, and no longer debate my points. If I have to hear one more teacher say, "That's very interesting, I'll have to give it further thought," I seriously think my head's going to explode.

I imagine that would really give this school something to talk about. I'd be Cody the Exploding-Headed Boy.

Throughout the morning I look constantly for Renee. I want to apologize for the hall incident and try to explain what really happened in the locker room. I think if I can just get her to listen to me, everything will be all right.

I don't see her until history class. She must be avoiding me; the school's large, but not that large. When I walk into the room I smile and try to get her attention, but she turns away and continues talking to her friend Fiona.

Everyone grows quiet, just like they have in all my other classes.

I take my seat and reach out and touch her shoulder. I whisper, "Hey, Renee, I'm sorry about this morning."

She doesn't look at me, she just mutters, "Whatever."

My voice grows a little louder. "I want to tell you what happened, you know, about the fight."

She sighs. "I don't want to talk about fights, and I thought I made it clear that I don't want to talk to *you*, either."

"Just let me explain what happened."

Her hand rises, signaling me to stop talking. "No. I don't want to hear it. Seriously."

I sink back into my seat and just let the class slip by. It's nothing new, just the same old history, with Mrs. Smith's strange twists. I watch Renee without being completely obvious. I don't want her to think I'm an obsessive freak or anything. She watches the teacher and doodles in her notebook. They're good doodles, too— cartoon figures, castles, flowing landscapes. I wonder if she paints. I bet she could paint a beautiful painting. Now that would be something worth hanging on one of my empty bedroom walls.

"Cody?"

I look at Mrs. Smith.

"Yes?"

I think I missed something. Everybody's staring at me.

"I asked you a question."

"I'm sorry. Could you repeat the question?"

She seems aggravated. "I said, is your group ready for its presentation?"

I give Renee and Fiona a questioning look. The three of us are working on a slide show about the important role France played in gaining our independence.

Renee rolls her eyes and Fiona shakes her head. We could do it, but they just don't want to. I'm not really in the mood, either.

I look at Mrs. Smith. She has her hand on her hip and a faraway expression like she'd rather be someplace else, maybe lying on a warm beach with her feet buried in the sand.

"I'm sorry. We're not ready yet. . . . Soon."

It looks like she's about to say something to me, then changes her mind. She addresses the class instead. "Are there any other groups that are ready?"

No one raises a hand.

"Okay, fine. Everybody split up into your groups for the remainder of the class. But, people, tomorrow is D-Day. I mean it. Presentations begin, so you had better be prepared."

The noise level drastically increases as everyone starts talking and moving desks together. I slide over to Renee and Fiona.

"I think we're ready for our presentation. Fiona, did you get those slides you were talking about?"

She ignores me.

"Come on, guys, we've got to work on this. Renee, I said I was sorry. What more do you want?"

Her soft brown eyes change; they become cold and hard. "I want you to leave me alone. That's what I want. Is that so difficult to understand?"

"Don't be like that." There's a pleading quality to my voice I've never heard before. "Give me a chance to at least tell you my side of the story."

"Cody, I don't want to hear it."

I sink down low in my desk and rest my chin on my crossed arms. I quietly watch the girls. Somehow they've made me disappear. It's like they cast a spell and I just vanished. All the countless hours I've spent mastering martial arts are useless against this kind of a fight.

They're talking about some TV show that was on last night. From their description it sounds totally absurd and like a complete waste of time.

Then the talk moves to how disappointed they were that the mice weren't set free.

Renee gets all worked up about how cruel it is to keep all those mice in cages. She proclaims that "mice were meant to be free."

I've been thinking a lot about this whole mice story and I just don't buy it. Everyone keeps talking about the "hundreds" of mice that are in the science lab. I've never seen any mice in there, and as far as I know nobody has ever used a mouse for any kind of school experiment. We don't have a college research lab; it's junior high.

I lean forward. "I think it's an urban legend."

Renee looks over at me with a surprised expression, like I suddenly dropped out of the sky and landed next to her. "What's an urban legend? What are you talking about?"

"This whole mice thing. I don't believe it."

"What's not to believe?"

"I don't believe that there are *hundreds* of mice in the science lab. Has anyone ever actually *seen* them?"

"I have." We both look at Fiona. Her eyes are wide with excitement. "They're in the science lab supply room. It looks like a scene out of a strange movie. Mr. Rizzo breeds them."

I can feel myself frowning. "Why would a science teacher breed mice?"

Fiona's getting more animated; this seems to be a topic she's given a great deal of time and consideration. "My mother, who works part time in the guidance office, says a lot of the teachers think that Mr. Rizzo is nuts. They call him the Mice Man."

"It still doesn't make sense to me. Why would the school allow him to breed mice?"

"Story is, the old science teacher requested a dozen for a maze experiment and now Mr. Rizzo's running a breeding and genetics experiment. There's a chart on the wall in the back of the class."

"I still don't believe it."

Renee lets out a long, exaggerated sigh. "What's not to believe? Do you think Fiona's lying?"

"I'm not saying that. I'm just saying that I don't believe it."

She mutters, "That figures. Why don't you go see if you can beat the truth out of somebody?"

Then the two of them cast that spell again and I become invisible. They continue their conversation about the cruel crime against nature being allowed to happen *right in our school* without anyone doing anything about it.

I've had enough.

I ask Mrs. Smith if I can use the bathroom and sign myself out. The thing is, you should always have a plan. When you don't have a plan everything becomes so much more involved. My dad used to say, "First with your head, then with your heart." He meant plan first, then act. Wise advice.

It seemed so simple but I was dealing with an unknown element and that can always be troublesome. Someone once said, "Never underestimate your opponent." That's also wise advice, especially if you're trying to put them into a bag. Which, may I add, is something that's far easier said than done.

Mrs. Smith glares at me when I sign myself back into the room. I record my time as five minutes instead of the actual fifteen. I slip back into my chair and pretend I'm reading my history book. I keep my hands in my lap.

Renee's looking at me oddly. "Where did you go?"

"Bathroom."

"Took you long enough."

I try to act casual. "Yeah, stomach, you know, must have been something I ate."

"Are you bleeding?"

"What?"

"Your face, your cheek and chin."

I reach up and touch my face. I look at my fingers; I am bleeding a little. "It's nothing. I'm fine."

Renee's eyes open wide. "My god! What happened to your hands?"

I look at them again. They're full of little cuts and scratches. Why wouldn't those little guys just stay in the bag and who would have thought they could move so incredibly fast?

Sharp little nails.

Sharp little teeth.

"Um, nothing. I just had a problem with . . . with the toilet-paper dispenser. It was broken and I tried to open it and . . . well."

"You were fighting again. Weren't you?"

"No! Really, I wasn't."

"Then how did you get so cut up?"

"I told you. Toilet-paper dispenser."

She throws up her hands in exasperation. "What? Do I *look* like an idiot? Who gets attacked by a toilet-paper dispenser?"

The bell rings.

I quickly stand up and start gathering my books. "I wasn't fighting."

Renee's packing her stuff, not even glancing in my direction. She mutters, "Whatever."

We're halfway out of class when we hear the first scream. It's followed by many, many more. We all rush to the open door.

Out in the hall, there are little white mice . . . *everywhere*.

DRAWING PATTERNS
IN THE DIRT

"So let me get this straight. You want to use *my* gym to teach *your* friends karate?"

I look Andy in the eye. I can't tell if he's actually mad or just giving me a hard time for the fun of it.

"Only if it's okay with you."

He stares off into the distance. I'm not sure why he's giving so much thought to a simple yes or no question.

"Okay, here's the deal: You can use the gym, but there are two conditions. Number one, everyone has to respect my gym, my house, and me."

"Of course."

"I don't want my gym becoming party central. Understand?"

"Understood."

"Number two, you and I need to have a long, honest talk about what's going on around here and what's this big secret you're carrying around about your past."

Now it's my turn to stare off into the distance. My dad told me the only person in this world I should trust is him. He taught me to hold my cards firmly against my chest, to never reveal anything, but then again, he also said I should *always* trust my gut.

Like it or not, Andy is caught up in whatever is going on around here and I'm going to have to tell him *something*. It's possible I'm even going to need his help. My gut tells me it's time to talk, but to be careful.

I decide to just plunge in. It's like swimming: If you spend too much time dipping your toes in the water, you never get in. "Okay."

"Okay what?"

"Okay, I'll tell you about my past, but only if you promise not to tell anyone."

He seems surprised. "I can agree to that. Let me get my sweatshirt. We can't do it here. I'll tell you why later."

"What about my friends?"

"You brought your friends? They're here now? You just assumed I would let them use my gym?"

"Um, yeah, I guess. Well, I didn't *bring* them. They came over after detention."

Andy rubs his eyes. He looks tired; maybe I woke him from a nap.

"Detention, huh? All of them had detention?"

"Yeah, but it was nothing serious—kind of my fault anyhow."

He starts to yawn, moves his shoulders and stretches his back; it really does seem like he just woke up. "Have you even taught anyone karate before?"

"Um, no, but I was wondering . . . maybe, um, I guess I've got some ideas."

He runs his hand through his hair and scratches the top of his head. "You've got some ideas? Maybe one of them was that I could help you?"

I smile. I try not to but it just tugs its way onto my face. "I was kinda hoping you could. That is, if you're not too busy."

For a moment it looks like he's thinking about going back into the house and shutting the door in my face. We just stand there on his porch. Finally he starts to grin and shakes his head.

"What is it about you? You have this way of bending people . . . Okay, tell you what: I'll give it a try. That's all I'll agree to. Why not? I haven't had any luck finding a job. I've got to do something more than watching TV and sleeping or I'm going to go out of my mind."

"Thank you."

"Don't thank me yet. I haven't done anything. Come on. Let's go meet your friends before I change my mind."

We walk around the side of the house and find them standing by the driveway. They all have their hands buried deep in their pockets. Some are kicking the ground and they don't seem to know what to do with their eyes.

Andy nods. "Hello, boys."

They mutter, "Hello, sir."

"Cody tells me he'd like to teach you karate in my personal gym. Is that right?"

They grunt "Uh-huh," nod their heads, and continue to avoid eye contact. Everyone seems very uncomfortable. Just to have something to do, I pick a broken branch off the driveway and toss it into the woods.

"Cody?"

Andy's looking at me with a strange expression. I'm not sure what I did wrong. "Yeah?"

"What happened to your hands?"

I glance at them. They actually look worse than they did this afternoon. The scratch marks are red and swollen. "Nothing."

I can hear the guys starting to snicker.

"No, really, what happened to your hands?"

"Um, I was playing football and I accidentally ran into a rose-bush."

Pogo Stick mumbles, "More like a hall full of mice."

They all start to snort and giggle, desperately trying not to laugh out loud.

I pretend I didn't hear anything. How did they know it was me?

I don't think Andy appreciates inside jokes. He seems annoyed. His voice rises and there's a sharp edge to it. "It doesn't matter *what* happened, all that matters is that you do something about it. You don't want that to get all infected, do you? When you get inside put some peroxide on it. Got it?"

"Okay."

He raises his chin at me. "Now, why don't you introduce your friends?"

"Um, sure, let's see, the tall guy, with the tape on his nose? That's Billy, but everyone calls him Pogo Stick. That's John, there's Jay and Rob—everyone calls him Bop, no one knows why—those two are the Gomez brothers, Jose and Carlos, and over there, under the basketball net, that's Frank."

Andy clears his throat and gives everyone a weak smile. He seems a little nervous but I'm not sure why. "Nice to meet you. I'm not good with names so you might have to remind me later. Although, I think I'll remember Pogo Stick and Bop. I'm sure Cody already told you but my name's Andy."

They all mutter hello.

"Let me show you the gym."

We follow him around to the back of the house. I watch Pogo Stick and John exchange glances. John smiles and pulls his hand up into his sleeve and acts like he's missing an arm.

Without turning around Andy says, "Guys, I lost an arm, not my eyes."

John's hand shoots down his sleeve and the smile disappears from his face. Pogo Stick grows serious and looks straight ahead. I'm about to laugh but manage to control myself.

The back door opens and we follow Andy into his basement. I watch the others for their reaction and I'm not surprised. From the outside it looks like just another normal house with just another basement, but once you walk through that door you cross into someplace special.

This time it's Frank who voices the thoughts of the group. "This place is so cool."

Andy seems pleased by their reactions. "Like I told Cody, you guys are welcome to use the gym as long as you treat it with respect. Think you can do that?"

They all nod.

"I've also agreed to help Cody teach self-defense techniques. I'm a trained instructor for the Army Rangers. I've served in Afghanistan and Iraq. If you guys are serious and willing to work hard I'll get you into the best shape of your life."

I'm surprised at how much effort everyone put into everything. I had expected Pogo Stick and the guys to give up after fifteen minutes but they all stuck with it. Especially Frank. I thought he'd be the first to quit, but the guy just kept plodding along.

In the beginning I tried to teach them but it didn't take the guys long to realize that Andy's a far better teacher than I am. It just seems to come natural for him. By the end of the class he was barking out orders to everyone and they pushed themselves really hard to please him. I think seeing what he could do with only one arm inspired them to give it their all. I even found myself pushing harder than normal.

One thing I did notice right away. They're going to need a whole lot of practice. Right now, I have serious doubts they'd be able to defend themselves against a Girl Scout troop.

It was a while before everyone left. No one seemed to want to go. A couple of the parents even had to come inside to get the guys. Pogo Stick's mother came in still wearing her uniform. I thought she was a nurse but Pogo said she's a dental hygienist. Bop's dad stayed the longest; he huddled in the corner talking to Andy.

Frank was the last to leave. He gave me a thumbs-up and a smile when he walked out the door. I'm glad he came. He joked a lot and added something to the group with his determination.

"Want one?" Andy's standing with a couple of cold water bottles in his hand.

"Sure." I take one, unscrew the cap, and guzzle half the bottle. I guess I was thirsty.

"I think it's time we had that talk."

I stare at my reflection in the mirror, T-shirt wet with sweat, water bottle in hand. I was prepared to tell him everything but now I'm wondering if that's the right thing to do. What if it somehow makes everything worse?

It's almost as if he reads my mind. "Don't worry. I just want to know what you've got me caught up in. What we talk about stays between you and me. I give you my word on that."

I blow out a long breath of air. I think about the man in black again. The way he glides through the woods, that huge gun he carries, the metal box. I'm tired of the constant paranoia, and why doesn't my dad call me? I feel like I'm floating in the middle of the ocean with nothing in sight. I'm sick of having to deal with all of this by myself. I need help.

I keep my eyes on my reflection. "If you want to talk, I'll talk, but you have to understand, it's tough for me."

A small degree of anger slips into his voice. "I get that, but it's important for *you* to understand that I *have to know* what's going on around here. Someone's checking up on one of us. One of us might be in a great deal of danger. For our own protection we have to first figure out who."

It never occurred to me that this might have something to do with Andy and nothing about me. But it could. That would explain why he hasn't tried to involve the police or someone else. Maybe Andy's got a secret he's hiding, too.

"Okay, let's talk. What do you want to know?"

He stands and slips his sweatshirt over his head. "Not here.

Let's go for a slow jog. We can talk while we run. Got to be careful."

We walk to the end of the driveway and take off down the street at a slow, even pace. At first, the sight of Andy jogging looks really strange to me. With only one arm there's no even flow; it's like watching a one-winged bird somehow fly.

When we're about a half a mile from the house I say, "So what do you want to know?"

"I guess for starters: Where do you come from? Where did you used to live?"

"All over."

"All over the country?"

"Not so much this country, mainly all over the world."

He glances at me. "Where in the world?"

"I guess I've been everywhere. All the continents except Antarctica, although we once spent a couple weeks in Ushuaia, Argentina, which is fairly close; it's the southernmost city in the world. I kind of liked it, although it was always cold and wet."

"Sure, right, but where's home? Where do you come back to?"

"Come back to? We don't come back to any particular place. It's just different hotels and rentals in different places, a week here, two weeks there. My dad says home is wherever we're together."

Andy jumps over a puddle of water. "So you're saying you never had a real home?"

"I guess."

"What about school?"

"My dad teaches me. We've got books. I'm almost done with high school. I've even studied a few college-level classes but they're kinda tough."

We run together in silence. Our bouncing shadows stretch before us like long, skinny giants. The thing is, I only studied one college class, political science; I don't know why I said a few. I shouldn't brag about something I didn't do. What if I'm asked which classes I've studied?

He looks over at me for a while. "Okay, now here's the big question. . . . What does your father do? And don't tell me the import-export business. I don't buy that."

I stare at the road in front of us. This is the moment I've dreaded—answer this question and you can never take it back. It will be out there forever. I watch my feet plodding along. Weighing the pros and cons of honesty. I decide to trust my gut. It's time to let the truth out.

"He works for the government. You know, like the CIA."

"He works for the CIA?"

"Yeah, and he lets me help. We work together, like a team."

"He does, huh? I've never known of . . . I guess what I mean is . . . that's highly unusual, the CIA letting him work with someone your age."

I begin to run a little faster. "Well, that's the way it's always been. You think I'm lying?"

"I didn't say that. Let me get this straight. He's been deep undercover all your life? Thirteen years? I've never known anyone who's been deep for that long."

I increase the length of my strides. "What's 'deep undercover' mean?"

"It means not reporting back to the central bureau. You assume an identity and then you wear it constantly."

"Well, that's us, I guess we're *deep undercover*."

Andy and I start breathing a little harder. In between breaths he says, "I've never known the CIA to work that way. They don't keep agents under that long."

I increase my speed even more. "Well, my dad's part of a secret branch of the CIA. A branch very few people know about."

The two of us are now close to a flat-out run. "Remember, I did some time . . . with military intelligence. I had . . . high clearance. Do you know the name . . . of this so-called secret branch? Maybe . . . I've heard of it."

"Of course I know the name! And there's . . . nothing *so-called* about it. It's real."

I don't know how much longer the two of us can keep up this pace. Andy rasps, "Okay . . . what's the . . . name . . . of this . . . group?"

I'm running even harder. I can barely talk. "It's . . . called . . . the . . . New Order."

"Ahhhh!" Andy suddenly stops running. It looks like he pulled something.

"Are you all right?" I stop and move to his side. "Where does it hurt?"

"I'm fine." He grabs my arm and looks me in the eye. "Did you say the New Order?"

"You've heard of the New Order?"

Andy glances up and down the street, then drags me into the woods. We stumble together through the thick brush, disappearing from sight. I follow him for about twenty feet before we sit on a rock near a slow-moving stream and catch our breath.

His voice sounds different, like a musical instrument that needs to be tuned. "You're not joking, right? You said the New Order?"

"Yeah. What's the matter? Have you heard of it?"

He picks up a stone, tosses it into the stream, and then just sits there watching the ripples flowing toward the shore. Finally he mutters, "I don't believe it."

"Believe what?"

"Tell me something. Is your father's first name Robert?"

"Yeah."

"How about your mother?"

"Her name was Jodi. But she was killed in Paris when I was almost two. I don't remember her."

He's quiet for a long time. When he talks his voice is flat and lifeless. "Everyone's looking for you."

"Looking for me? Who's looking for me? Who's everyone?"

I glance at Andy. He looks anxious. "The New Order—I don't believe it. You're legendary. If you get a bunch of high-level intelligence types out for a night on the town, the talk will always, eventually, turn to the New Order. Some people think your dad's a hero, others think he's a crazy vigilante."

My elbow jerks sideways and smashes into Andy's cheek. He falls backward onto the soft, damp earth. I jump off the rock, pin him to the ground, ball my hands into fists and shout, "He's not crazy! Take that back!"

He yells, "I didn't say he was! Calm down! Don't make me hurt you!"

Just as quickly as my anger overtook me it slips away. I roll off of Andy onto the ground beside him. I lie on my back and look at the trees stretching upward in the dense woods. Their leaves are changing, turning color, finally showing the first signs of the approaching autumn.

I glance at Andy. His cheek looks like it's starting to swell. "I'm sorry."

He's quiet for a while. "That's okay. No big deal. I've been hit harder before . . . by a bus."

The two of us start to laugh but it's a low, tired laugh. After a while I sit up and I'm surprised by the heavy sigh that escapes from me. I sound like Jenny. She's always sighing about something. I don't want it to hang in the air too long so I blurt out, "Tell me what you know about my father."

Andy's still lying on his back behind me. In a calm, steady voice with little emotion he says, "I'll tell you what I've heard, and this is just what I've *heard* so if it's wrong don't hit me . . . okay?"

I smile. "Okay."

"I guess I don't know that much but everyone's heard of him, well, that is, everyone in military intelligence. He used to work in the agency with his wife until she was killed in the line of duty."

I interrupt him. "That was my mother, Aunt Jenny's sister."

He swats at a few bugs flying around his head. "Yeah, I guess. Sorry. I heard your dad took it really hard and left the agency. He formed a group called the New Order."

I glance over at Andy. "So you're saying my dad *isn't* with the CIA anymore?"

"No, as far as I know he's on his own."

I'm not sure what to say about this. My dad's *always* told me we work for the CIA. What if Andy's right? It's not like I ever met anyone my dad works with. Could we be on our own?

The bugs seem to be getting more aggressive. Andy smacks one that landed on his leg. "The New Order claims they're trying to stop wars. Your dad's been plucking bad people out of bad situations before they can contribute to a war breaking out. Sometimes it even works."

"What's wrong with that?"

"I didn't say anything was wrong with it. I'm just telling you what I've heard, remember? Look at me. I'm the one-armed man who can't sleep at night. Do I look like a poster child for the glories of war?"

I turn around and glare at Andy. "Why is everyone looking for us? It sounds like what my dad's doing is a good thing."

His voice rises. Irritation slips into it. "Because war isn't simple, it's complicated, and sometimes it's even necessary. War can bring change. Sometimes change is good."

I think of something. "Are you saying it was the CIA who tried to kill us?"

"Someone tried to kill you?"

I tell him about the café bombing.

He stares off into the woods after I tell him the story. It's starting to get dark. "I could be wrong, but that doesn't sound like the CIA. They wouldn't risk killing that many people; it could lead to far greater problems. Sounds more like the work of terrorists or some independent militant group. Has your dad gone up against someone recently who doesn't work for any particular country?"

There's so many different places we've been and so many people we've *studied* that it's hard to even remember who's who, but then something pops into my head.

"We broke up this arms dealer selling weapons in South America but I doubt it could have been him. My dad didn't think much of him. He said he was some 'lowlife wiseguy' working out of New York."

Andy's eyes seem to open a little wider. "You do know 'wiseguy' is another way of saying someone who works for the mob, don't you?"

I shake my head no.

"Don't you watch TV?"

"Why does everyone keep asking me that? No, I don't watch TV."

Andy smiles. "Okay, the bottom line is this: Someone's after you and your dad but you don't know who?"

"Right. My dad just said that someone's after us and he has to take care of it. That's why I'm here. He didn't think it was safe for me to be with him."

"I know you don't want to hear it but he's probably right."

I pick up a large rock and toss it into the stream. Why couldn't my dad have had a normal job? I hate all of this.

I look over at Andy. He's drawing patterns in the dirt with a stick.

"Andy?" He looks up. "Are you going to tell anyone about me?"

He doesn't say anything, just continues to draw in the dirt. When I start to think that he didn't hear me he says, "I should . . . what your father is doing is dangerous. One mistake could be disastrous. I understand what he's trying to do—a part of me even admires it—but that doesn't make what he's doing right."

"So you're . . . going to tell?"

He blows out a long breath of air. "I gave you my word."

I can't help smiling. "Thank you."

"Don't thank me yet. We still have to figure out who's in the woods. My guess is that it's someone after your dad; they're probably watching you hoping he'll show up. I think you're safe as long as your dad stays away, but if things change and get too crazy around here, I just might have to call for some help. Oh, and there's one more thing."

I shake my head. I hate "one more things." They're *always* bad news. "What?"

"Remember the metal box in the woods? The one you saw the man in black remove? I found another one. It's a wireless camera. We're being watched."

"What? This is so messed up! What happened? Did you get rid of it?"

He quickly shakes his head. "No, I figure it's better if they think we don't know about it. Another thing to keep in mind is that if we're being watched, maybe we're also being bugged. So watch what you say."

I toss another rock into the stream. "Great, just great."

Andy stands up. "Hey, we'll figure something out. At least we know something's going on. That's to our advantage."

"I guess." I look around. It's dark. "Maybe we should head back."

"Right." He swats another bug. "Besides, these gnats are driving me crazy."

We stumble through the woods up to the road and start walking toward the house. I'm tired. I feel like I've been drained of all my energy.

I hear a car coming up the road behind us. It has a loud, powerful engine and the music is really pumping. I don't pay it much mind until it roars past us and slams on its brakes. I quickly look around for potential weapons. I see four.

A girl calls out, "Hey, guys! Whatcha doing?"

I relax a little as we walk toward the car. It's a convertible with its top down. Two girls are in the front seat. When we get closer I realize it's Renee and her sister, Annie. Annie's sitting behind the wheel with a huge smile plastered on her face.

She waves at Andy. "Hey, stranger. What are you doing out here?"

"Cody and I went out for a jog."

Renee calls out, "Hey, Cody! Liberator of mice. Defender of the just."

I wave and try to smile. She's a lot friendlier than this afternoon.

Annie puts her elbow on the door and leans toward us. "Hop in the back. I'll give you a ride."

Andy shows her our clothes. "Nah. Thanks, but we're a mess. We better walk."

"Don't be a jerk. Get in the car."

"But—"

"Guys, just get in the car. I'm not taking no for an answer."

We both hop into the backseat. Renee's giving me a big smile. I guess freeing the mice got me back on her good side.

Annie turns around. "You guys like ice cream?"

We nod our heads.

"Good, because we're kidnapping both of you. Next stop, the Ice Cream Shack."

The car roars off down the road. Renee turns up the music. Mailboxes fly by. Above us, spread out like a blanket, is the night sky. I see the very first star of the evening.

I make a wish.

VORTEX

"Cody, where were you? It's late!"

Jenny's sitting at the kitchen table in her robe, drinking a cup of herbal tea. The clock above the sink says ten past ten.

"Sorry. Andy and I got kidnapped."

"Kidnapped? What are you talking about? Who kidnapped you?"

"Annie and Renee Carrington. They said they would give us a ride home but they kidnapped us instead. They made us eat ice cream, told us jokes, and flirted. It was terrible. I'm sure I'll be . . . traumatized for life."

"Don't make me laugh. I'm mad at you. I've been worried. I didn't know what to do."

I sit next to her. "Sorry. I didn't think you'd worry. You know I can take care of myself."

Her voice rises, taking me by surprise. "Well, I did worry, and it doesn't matter if you can take care of yourself, you're still only thirteen. You let me know where you are. Do you hear me? If you're going to live here I at least want some respect."

I hold up my hands. "Hey, I didn't think it would be such a big deal. Besides, I don't have a cell phone."

"Come on. Are you telling me *no one* had a cell phone you could borrow? I don't believe that."

She's right. "I messed up. I should have called. Next time, okay? I promise."

I stand to leave but she reaches for my arm and pulls me back into the chair. "Not so fast, mister. You're not leaving this table until you tell me how it went with Renee, and I want details."

I do. A little at first, like an old-fashioned hourglass, but then I open up, and everything just spills out of my mouth. I tell her every detail from the moment they picked us up until we were dropped off, and it feels great. Jenny and I talk together for more than an hour. She tells me stories about when she was in school, guys she liked, things they did together.

She tells me about a date where everything went horribly wrong. I can't stop laughing and I find myself thinking, *I guess this is what it would be like to have a mother*. I like the way it feels. It's a lot different than the way my dad and I are together. It's somehow easier, like breathing at sea level instead of high in the mountains.

She gives me a long, tight hug and a kiss on the forehead before I go off to bed. It has that strange way of making me feel safe. I'm not sure how or why. It just does.

Sleep comes slow. I lie in bed waiting for it like an overdue bus. I can't believe this day. There's so much to think about—my dad, Renee, the karate class, the mice—but I'm also exhausted. I can't lie here and think about everything. It's suffocating. Eventually I slip away and fall into a dream.

My dad and I are sitting together someplace in India at a small outdoor café. It's hot and dusty. I'm bent over a plate eating a dish of the sweet, spicy ice cream type dessert called Kulfi. It's one of my favorites. I love it. I can actually eat it until it makes me sick.

My dad's looking at me. When I meet his eyes he smiles and says something but I don't understand what he's saying. It's in a language I've never heard before.

"What?"

He repeats what he said but I still don't understand him.

"What? I don't understand. Speak English."

He's getting aggravated but I don't know what he wants. I can't understand him. He's annoyed and I'm frustrated. We're two half bridges that don't meet in the middle.

Buzzzz.

Buzzzz.

I open my eyes. What's that sound? I look at the clock: 2:47.

Buzzzz.

Buzzzz.

It's coming from the kitchen. I spring out of bed and slip down the hall, rubbing the sleep out of my eyes. I'm ready for anything.

Buzzzz.

Buzzzz.

On the kitchen table Jenny's cell phone is vibrating. I pick it up and read "unknown caller." I flip it open before it buzzes again.

"Hello?"

"Cody?"

"Dad?"

"How are you, son?"

"Dad, it's three o'clock in the morning!"

"I know. I can't always pick and choose when to call. Now's the best time but we have to make it quick."

In the background I can hear the same sound I heard last time. It sounds like a machine that's crunching rocks, turning boulders into marbles.

I raise my voice. "Is everything okay? How's our problem?"

"Progress is being made but I need you to do something."

"What?" I'm surprised he can hear me over all that noise.

"You have to keep your eyes open. Understand?"

"I think so."

There's irritation in his voice. "Do you or don't you understand?"

"I do. I know what you mean."

"I hope so."

"Dad, is something wrong?"

"No, there's nothing to worry about, everything's under control. I'm finally close to putting an end to all this. I've set the wheels in motion. I want you to stay alert just in case."

"Okay."

The noise in the background suddenly gets louder, drowning out any thought of either one of us talking. When it gets back to the normal volume he says, "So how's school?"

It's tough for me to change topics like this but I manage to push myself forward. "It's good. Easy, though, stuff we covered years ago. I think I'm making friends."

"That's good news."

I think about what Andy told me. "Dad?"

"Yes, son."

"Do we really work for who you said we do?"

There's a long moment of silence. I start to wonder if he's still there. Finally he says, "Cody, everything's just the way I told you. I have to go now."

"Dad, can't you talk just a little longer?" I can't believe he has to go already.

"Sorry, I can't. Soon, though, okay?"

"Dad . . ." The call disconnects.

I mutter, ". . . I miss you."

Once again I'm left standing in the kitchen with a cell phone pressed uselessly against my ear. I don't know why but my eyes tear up. I'm just getting so frustrated. I don't want to be part of this whole saving-the-world routine anymore. I want a normal life with all the boring normal things that come with it, like a full night's sleep, school, friends, and a dad who's got a nine-to-five job.

I'm so tired.

The light blazes on. I'm not sure how Jenny managed to walk down the hall without me hearing her. It must have been all that noise on the phone. She's standing there in her nightgown; her hair pushed this way and that.

"Is everything okay? Who were you talking to?"

The light's so bright that it hurts my eyes. I blink and wipe at them with the backs of my hands.

"Cody, hon, are you crying?"

I turn my back to her. I try to hide my frustration but my voice betrays me. "No, I'm . . . fine. Really. You know, it's just . . . the light."

She places her hand on my shoulder. "Was that your dad?"

"Yeah."

"Is everything okay?"

"I dunno. I guess."

She turns me around, gives me a little smile before wiping my cheek. Then she pulls me close. "I'm sorry, Cody. I'm sure everything will eventually work out."

When I round the corner I'm surprised to see Albert. Not that it's unusual for him to be at the bus stop; in fact, he always seems to get there first. No, what surprises me is that he's wearing a suit. It looks like it's cheap, something off the rack, and the tie doesn't really match, but it definitely counts as a suit. I personally think it's a vast improvement over his old baggy clothes.

I stand next to him, nod my head in approval, and smile. "Nice suit."

"Yeah, not as nice as yours, but I kinda like it."

"I can see why."

He looks down and kicks a small stone. "Hey, I was wondering. Would you mind if I joined your after-school karate class?"

"Of course, that would be great! You didn't have to ask. I just assumed that if you wanted to be a part of it you would come on down."

Cell Phone Girl is shaking her head as she approaches us. "I don't believe it. Now there's two of you? What is this, some kind of twisted psycho cult with an extreme dress code?"

She's standing next to me with a big smile. I don't understand. Yesterday she seemed terrified to be anywhere near me and today she's acting like we're old friends.

She places her backpack next to mine and holds out her small hand. "Um, I don't know if I ever told you, but my name's Debbie."

I shake her hand. I'm amazed at how fragile and delicate it feels. I could easily break the bones if I tried. "I'm Cody."

"I know. I think what you did was the coolest thing ever."

"What did I do?"

"You know, freeing the mice? I don't know who made that YouTube video with the puppet but it's the funniest thing I've seen all year. I must have watched it twenty times."

"Someone made another video of me?"

"Yes! You mean you haven't seen it? It's hysterical. There's this cute little puppet wearing a suit and tie. He stuffs all these tiny mice into a bag and then releases them in the hall. They run all over the place. You gotta see it."

"I guess."

The bus pulls up. I'm not even at the top of the stairs when Troy Sampson is barking out my name again. He's saving me the same seat he did before.

When I get closer I realize he's wearing a tie under his leather jacket. He smiles and holds up the tie. "I kind of like the way this looks. Somehow it makes me seem smarter. Maybe a couple of my teachers will finally give me a break."

Albert keeps muttering, "I hate that guy," but he winds up sitting next to him anyway while I'm across the aisle. Troy can be very persuasive.

Much to my surprise, Albert and Troy spend the whole ride to school talking about baseball. The World Series has been going on all week. You just can't escape it. The New York Yankees are playing the New York Mets. It seems like that's a really big deal around here. It's become this gate that every conversation has to pass through.

Amber and Nicki squeeze into my seat and chatter nonstop about the YouTube video. It doesn't matter how many times I tell them I never saw it, they just keep talking and talking about it. They say I make a very cute puppet.

Once again school is a welcome sight. I hate riding the bus.

Frank, Pogo Stick, and the rest of the karate club are waiting for me just inside the front door. For some reason I'm not really surprised when I see that they're all dressed neatly and wearing ties.

We stand in the front hall talking. Almost everyone who walks through the door turns and stares at us.

There are some other groups of kids in the front hall. It's a common meeting place. I've seen people meeting here every day. You meet, you talk, you move along together to homeroom.

Steroid Steve marches over to our group with that odd way of walking he has. It's like he's carrying a large barrel under each arm and squeezing a third between his thighs.

He barks, "Hey, you guys gotta move along! No gang activity is allowed in the school."

I start to laugh. "What are you talking about? We're not a gang. We're just dressed up."

His voice grows louder. "You're dressed alike and congregating together—that constitutes suspicious gang activity."

I'm really getting tired of this guy. That roundhouse kick is way overdue.

Troy steps forward and pats me on the back. "Forget about it. I once watched Steve-O here break up a troop of '*suspicious*' Girl Scouts. The guy's clueless. Let's just get going."

Troy and Steroid Steve glare at each other. It's obvious that there's a long dark history between the two of them.

We walk away and head on down the hall. It's almost like we're moving in slow motion. Everyone turns and watches us parade by. Maybe there's more to what Steve was saying than I gave him credit for.

Each day I notice more and more kids wearing ties to school. At first it's friends of friends, but then I start noticing kids wearing ties that have no connection to us. It's strange how some things grow without much effort. Like my karate club, which seems to pick up more kids every day.

Andy also agreed to be Bop's father's personal trainer. Within a week he had four more clients. All of them willing to pay big bucks to have an Army Ranger rant and yell at them to push themselves harder.

We're all sitting on the cold, damp grass.

"Frankfurter!"

"Yes, Coach?"

"Same drill. Start your lap."

Frank reluctantly rises to his feet and starts plodding along.

I stand up. "Coach?"

"You have something to say, Teacup?"

"Yes, Coach. We've decided we're not going to do this to Frank anymore."

"And what's that, Teacup?"

"This whole 'pass him so he has to take another lap' routine."

Coach Dinatelli glares at me. I think he expects me to get nervous and back down. Finally he says, "Well, Teacup, it's not up to you to decide what we do or don't do in *my* class."

I glare right back at him. "And another thing. We don't like your stupid nicknames. If you expect to be addressed in a certain manner we deserve the same consideration. How would you like it if we started calling you Coach Blowhard?"

Mrs. Owens taps her fingernails slowly on her desk. "Congratulations, Mr. Saron. I think you've established a new school record."

I let a long moment of silence pass us by. It's become our accustomed manner of communicating. Words followed by long pauses. "What record would that be?"

"Student with the most teacher complaints. Usually that honor goes to someone with a severe hygiene problem."

I smile. I'm starting to appreciate Mrs. Owens's sense of humor. It grows on you. She'll never do stand-up but it can work well with a small captive audience of one.

"Do I get a trophy?"

She raises her eyebrows. That's about as close to a smile as you'll ever receive from her. "No, but that's an interesting idea. Something to take into consideration."

"Um, Mrs. Owens, may I say something about Coach Dinatelli's complaint?"

She holds up her hand. "Let me finish reading it." She reads through the page. Her eyes rise briefly. "Coach Blowhard?"

"Well, it's like—"

She stops me again with her hand and continues to read.

When she finishes, she places the sheet of paper in a growing file with my name on it. "What class do you have now, Mr. Saron?"

"Um, Spanish."

"See Miss Reed at the front desk for a late pass."

I stand up. "But what about the complaint?"

She walks around her desk and holds open the door for me. "Sometimes, the underdog wins."

"So, I'm not in trouble?"

"Not today." Her eyebrows rise. "At least, not yet. You still have a few hours left."

Were you in the woods last night?"

Andy signals that I should lower my voice. He's worried about bugs, but I point at the CD player; it's loudly pumping out music. It would be impossible to record anything while it's blasting.

Still, when he talks his voice is so low I can barely hear it. "I was out early in the evening—was that you that I heard around midnight?"

I shake my head. "No. You heard it too?"

"How could I not? Our friend is getting loud. For some reason that worries me."

"I know what you mean."

Andy gestures that I should follow him and we walk across the gym to the storage closet. He squats down and opens a box. I peer inside. "What is it?"

He grins and talks almost directly into my ear. "I called an old buddy of mine. I think it's time we start fighting fire with fire. It's a wireless camera of our own, two of them actually, with night-vision capacity, and this is a silent driveway alarm system. We can set it up in the woods. When he trips the beam we'll know where he is."

Now it's my turn to grin. "Now you're talking."

Hey, guys." I place my lunch tray at the end of the table. Most of the karate club is here. We've fallen into the habit of sitting at the same table everyday.

"Cody! I've got to ask you something."

Why does Pogo Stick always talk with a mouth full of food? I turn my head slightly so I don't have to look at the contents of his lunch. "What's up?"

"Frank tells me you've got a thing for Renee Carrington, that right?"

I look at my plate and start moving things around with my fork. I can feel my face getting hot. I hope it's not turning red. "I don't know."

He slaps Bop on the back. "Ha! Told ya. That's a yes."

I plead with Pogo. "Come on. Give me a break."

"Hey, I'm not giving you a hard time. Renee's cute. Is she going to the dance next week?"

"Um . . . I don't know."

Pogo thinks for a moment, then calls across the table, "Frank, Frank." He's talking with the Gomez brothers about the World Series. "Frank!"

Frank looks over at us. "What?"

"Renee Carrington's friend. The little redheaded thing."

"You mean Fiona?"

"Yeah, that's it, Fiona. She lives on your street, right?"

Frank takes a sip of his milk. "Yeah, like three houses down. Nice girl."

"She at your bus stop?"

"Yeah, why?"

"Could you ask her if Renee's going to the dance?"

He shrugs. "Sure, why not."

Pogo turns to me and smiles. "There you are. I bet she'll be there."

I push around my food for a while before confessing. "I've never been to a dance before. What are they like?"

"What are they like? It's time for you to get out of your cave. Hang with us. We'll be over by the clock."

Cody, I wanted to catch you before history."

Renee's standing in the hall with the oddest expression. I can't get a read on it. I look into her eyes: she seems nervous. I think she has bad news.

"Something wrong?"

"No. Well, kinda. I just want to ask you something."

"What?"

She touches my shoulder. "Not here, okay? But I want to know if I can drop by your house tomorrow. You've got your karate club going on, right?"

Why did she touch my shoulder? That's the type of thing you do when you feel sorry for someone. Maybe she thinks I've been getting too friendly. Maybe she wants me to back off. Did Frank say something to her?

"Cody?"

"Huh?"

"So . . . can I? Can I stop by?"

"Yes, of course. Stop by anytime. Vegetarians are always welcome."

She's not even smiling. This has got to be really bad news.

The worst part of waking up in the morning is the getting-out-of-bed part. Not that I've got anything against getting out of bed; it's perfectly fine if that's what you choose to do.

Today it's easy to get out of bed. Today, I can smell Jenny's pancakes. When she whips up and fries that batter, creating those delicious little golden cakes, now *that's* something I choose to get out of bed for.

I hurry into the kitchen. "Mmmm, something smells great and it's not even the weekend. I love it!"

Jenny's wearing an old pair of sweats, huge slippers that look like furry feet, and a New York Mets baseball cap.

"Hey, I thought you were a Yankees fan."

"I told you that was just a hat. I picked this hat up because you said you hated the Yankees. Tonight's the big night. Game seven. Whoever wins tonight will be the champs, so . . . let's go, Mets!"

I wave my finger in the air, aggravation slipping into my voice. "*Ooooh!* Ask me if I care. Really, what is it with people around here? You'd think the fate of the free world depended on this stupid game."

Jenny holds up her hands. "Whoa . . . put that monster back

in its box. People work hard, if they want a little diversion, what's the big deal?"

"I guess."

She sits down next to me. "Guess what? Your mother loved baseball."

"Really?"

"Yeah, we used to go to the games with our dad. I had a good time but your mom . . . she loved it."

"What was her favorite team?"

She smiles. "I think it was the Mets, but she'd go to any game. Mainly she just loved going to the ballpark, you know, the hot dogs, the ice cream . . . the boys."

Jenny gives me one of those sideways glances like a shoplifter thinking she's getting away with something. "And as long as we're on that subject, how's Renee?"

Her question doesn't bother me today, and I'm about to say "fine" but instead I find myself blurting out, "I don't know. I'm worried; she wants to talk to me about something after my karate club. I get the feeling she wants me to stop talking to her."

She places a hand on my shoulder. "Don't worry. If she were going to tell you she didn't want to talk to you, she'd just *tell* you she doesn't want to talk. She wouldn't make an appointment. That doesn't make a whole lot of sense. Think about it."

"I guess."

"I'm betting it's either something good or it's something that has nothing to do with you. And you know what I want?"

"What?"

"When you find out, I want to be the first to know. Okay?"

"Okay."

"Now, eat your pancakes. How about some orange juice?"

She walks over to the refrigerator and pulls out the carton.

"Sure. . . . And, Jenny?" She glances over her shoulder. "Thanks for everything. You've been great."

Her eyes light up. "Oh, hon, thank you. I love having you here. When you live and work by yourself you tend to get set in your ways. Thanks for making my life more . . . interesting."

I looked for Renee all day long. I was sure she was avoiding me. It wasn't until history started and her chair remained empty that I realized she just wasn't in school.

All through the karate class I keep one eye on the back door, expecting to see her smiling face any second. It's all I want right now, everything else can wait. It's so strange. There's the café bombing and everything that followed in its path, there's all this crazy, life-threatening stuff that I should be thinking about, but right now all I can think about is Renee.

I keep pushing the class, not wanting it to end, not wanting to give up on Renee.

"Okay!" Andy steps forward. "I think that's enough for today."

The guys practically collapse on the mats.

Pogo Stick moans, "Man, Cody, what are you trying to do, kill us?"

Andy starts handing out water bottles. "I think Cody wants to be a drill sergeant. He's trying to turn all of you into lean, mean, fighting machines."

I smile but it's mainly to hide my embarrassment. I didn't realize I was pushing everyone that hard. They look exhausted.

Bop guzzles his water and goes to the refrigerator for another. He twists off the top and says, "Andy, can I ask you something?"

"Sure."

"How'd you lose your arm?"

I can't believe he just asked that. Maybe that's something Andy doesn't want to talk about. Didn't he think about that? I glance around the room: everyone looks as uncomfortable as I feel.

"Oh, my arm? I lost it in Iraq."

Pogo Stick surprises me by saying, "How?" Not that I blame him. I think everyone in the room wanted to say that word. He just had less self-control than the rest of us.

Andy smiles but it isn't one of those happy smiles, it's more of an I'll-smile-just-because smile. "So, you want to hear a war story?"

Pogo Stick nods his head.

"Okay, then." He lets out a long breath of air. "Let's see, I guess you could say a teddy bear took my arm."

I heard "teddy bear" but it didn't really make sense to me. My mind keeps repeating the sentence. Shuffling the words around, searching for a new meaning that makes some kind of sense.

John asks in a voice that sounds very little like his normal one, "Did you say . . . teddy bear?"

"Yes. We were on foot patrol in Baghdad heading back to camp and we were just at that point where you start to relax a little. Not a lot, because you never really relax, but just a little. These thoughts of what you're going to do later start popping into your head."

Andy takes a long pull from his water bottle. I notice that it's shaking in his hand.

"Anyhow, we went around a corner and came upon this teddy bear lying on the sidewalk. It was . . . well, I guess you'd call it 'cute,' something you'd see back home. One of the guys went to pick it up, I told him to leave it alone but he picked it up anyway. There was this noise, it sounded like a big kid belly-flopping into a pool, followed by a really bright flash; it was like looking into the sun. It blinded me; I couldn't see a thing."

He stops talking. Beads of sweat are running down his forehead. He closes his eyes for a second, takes a deep breath, and pushes on with the story.

"I don't remember much after that, just being terrified, bullets and grenades were flying all around. I was running blind, with one hand outstretched and the other on the wall of a building, feeling my way for cover until an explosion lifted me off my feet and slammed me down in a dirt alleyway."

The room is silent. We all look at one another. Something about the way Andy told the story made me feel like I was there. I think the others felt it too. It was in his eyes. I could see the fear, the confusion, and the pain. Maybe my dad's right: maybe it is time to try to end war.

John clears his throat. "Um, did the explosion take your arm off?"

"I was in a coma for three days. When I woke, it was gone."

Pogo Stick asks, "Was that scary? I mean, when you woke up and realized your arm was gone."

Andy's quiet for a long time, just leaning against the wall, looking at the floor. I start to wonder if we might have asked him one too many questions.

Finally he looks up and says, "More than you can ever imagine."

The room's quiet, the CD ended long before Andy started to talk. Now the silence seems suffocating. I'd like to say something, anything, to fill this emptiness but nothing comes to mind.

Knock.

Knock.

Knock.

Everyone jumps, even Andy. I look at the door. Renee's outside with a huge smile, energetically waving through the window at us.

The guys start to tease me. I think it's mainly just something to throw into the air, a welcome opportunity to escape from the silent aftermath of Andy's story.

I don't mind, I'm glad to see her and I'd rather hear a chorus of "*Oooh*, it's Cody's girlfriend" than the vicious silence that was just smothering us moments before.

I jog across the room and meet her outside. "Hey, I was worried you weren't going to show up."

She smiles. "Sorry, it's my sister. She's running late for everything."

"That's okay, at least you made it. Want to come in and say hello to the guys?"

She stops smiling. "No. Is there someplace we can go to talk? It's kinda important."

I try to keep an upbeat tone to my voice. I tell myself that whatever happens, no matter how bad her news is, I won't let her see how disappointed I am.

"Sure, there's a bench over by the apple tree."

We walk across the backyard and sit side by side on the bench. It's a warm fall night; the sun's setting behind us, and the sky is a blazing canopy of colors. If I wasn't expecting bad news this could be a perfect romantic moment.

I look into her eyes. They look so sad. "Renee, what's the matter?"

"It's my sister."

"Is everything okay?"

"No, it's Johnny."

"What? Who's Johnny?"

She takes a big breath. "Johnny's my sister's boyfriend. Remember? He's in the army?"

I nod my head. "Oh, yeah."

"Well, they've been dating, like, forever, ever since high school, they were even talking about getting married. They had all this history, all these plans."

"Did something happen to Johnny in Iraq?"

"You could say that. It really changed him, turned him into a different person. Mean and nasty. He used to be so nice. I noticed it the last time he was in town. A few days ago he called my sister and told her he didn't want to see her anymore. Just like that. He said he met someone new. I guess she's in the army, too."

I shake my head. "That's messed up. How's your sister?"

"She's a wreck. She hasn't been to work, she doesn't sleep, hardly eats. The thing is, I know she worried about him every day he was over there. Every single day, think about that. Then to have him just leave her like this? It's . . . it's too much for her."

I have her hand in mine. I'm not sure how that happened, she just reached out while she was talking and they folded together. "Anything I can do to help?"

She looks me in the eye. "Funny you should say that. I've got this idea. It's something you can help me with."

"What would you like me to do?" Sitting here on this bench,

with her hand in mine, I believe I would do absolutely anything she suggested, even if she wanted me to go to Iraq and personally kidnap Johnny.

There's a little gleam to her eyes. "It's like this: I know my sister likes Andy and it's easy to see how much Andy likes my sister. Maybe the four of us should do more things together. Like we did last week at the Ice Cream Shack. We don't have to push, just put them together and see what happens."

"I think that's a great idea. You had me worried, I thought you were coming here to tell me to back off."

"Back off?"

"You know, I thought maybe I was becoming a pest or something."

She quickly leans forward and kisses me on the lips. It happens so fast I don't even have time to react. "You're definitely not a pest. I want to do more things with you, not less."

Did she really just kiss me? On the lips? Why didn't I kiss her back? I don't believe it, my first kiss was over before I even realized what was happening. Figures.

Say something. You're just sitting here. She's going to think you're really strange if you just sit here. Say something. "Um, I want to do more with you too."

She rests her hand on my shoulder. "How about now? Annie's waiting in her car. You think you could get Andy? We'll all go out for pizza."

"Sounds good to me, but let me ask Jenny. I'm sure she'll say yes but I have to ask her first. Then I'll work on Andy."

"All right, I'll meet you over by the car."

I jump to my feet and run to our cottage. I think I set a new record for covering the two hundred feet. I burst through the front door.

"Hey, Jenny!"

I slam the door behind me.

"Jenny! You were right!"

I run down the hall toward the kitchen.

"Jenny, you'll never guess what just . . ."

She's in the middle of the kitchen, tied to a chair, duct tape covering her mouth. She grunts, moans, tries to say something. Her eyes are wide, full of panic and fear.

I hear someone behind me.

I pivot on my left foot. A large man is thundering toward me, at least twice my size.

I snap kick, aiming for his throat but he's moving too fast, and I catch him in the chest. He stumbles back. I sweep his left knee and it buckles slightly.

My hand shoots out, fingers stiff, going for his eyes. I only catch one but it's enough to get me in close with a jab, cross, and an elbow strike across his chin. He's stunned; I step back to ready a roundhouse to his temple.

But he's fast; he's on top of me and slams me against the wall.

I hear a crash as something smashes to the floor. I get in another quick shot at his left knee. It buckles more this time and he grunts. I move inside with a jab and cross to his nose; I feel it break with the second punch.

He howls in pain, picks me up by my throat, and slams me down on the kitchen table. It collapses onto the floor. Everything goes black for a second. Everything hurts. I roll to the side as he thunders after me and I grab a table leg off the floor. I slam it against that left knee again. It buckles all the way this time.

I've got him.

I spring to my feet. I've got a clear shot at his head.

"Hold it!"

There's someone behind me. I look over my shoulder. There's another large man hurrying into the kitchen. He's pointing an AK-47 at me. The huge weapon has my full attention.

"Drop it!"

I let the table leg fall to the floor.

He keeps the gun pointed at me and barks at the other guy, "Didn't I tell you to be careful with the kid? Told you he was a weapon!"

The guy I was fighting grabs a kitchen towel and presses it against his bleeding nose. "I think the little punk broke my nose!"

He spits a mouthful of blood into the sink. "And he messed up my knee big-time."

"You're just lucky I got back in time. One more second and he would have taken you out."

He spits into the sink again. "I don't know about that. I had the punk lined up."

The gunman aims the rifle at my chest. "Yeah, right. Tie him up tight and tape his mouth and eyes. Do her eyes, too."

Broken Nose Guy slams me down in a kitchen chair. I make eye contact with Jenny. She looks terrified. I try to smile. My arms are pulled behind me and my wrists are bound with rope.

I hear him pull a piece of duct tape off the roll and rip it. A moment later he slaps it across my mouth. He repeats the process for my eyes but this time he really slaps the tape on hard. It's like being punched one last time.

Gunman says, "Were the lights off in the main house before?"

"I dunno, I think so."

Someone's ripping another piece of duct tape.

"Doesn't matter. Let's go. But keep your eyes open."

I'm pulled to my feet. I hear the same being done to Jenny. "Okay, guys, here's the deal. We're going to go out the back door, through the woods, to a van parked on the road. If anyone tries anything funny, the other one gets shot. Nod your head if you understand."

I nod my head. I'll cooperate. I don't want anything to happen to Jenny.

What's Renee going to think when I don't come back?

It felt like we drove for hours. We were thrown into the rear of a van and we slid around on the hard metal floor like two sacks of flour. I managed to inch my bound body over to Jenny's and pressed myself up against her. It kept us from sliding and gave me some comfort to feel her next to me.

The two men, who called each other "Dude" and "Dawg," listened to the World Series as we bounced along on the back roads. Dawg was the one whose nose I broke; he complained about it constantly. What a wimp.

They cheered loudly and pounded on the dashboard every time the Yankees scored a run. Figures.

I managed to roll over Jenny and get behind her. The radio was so loud they didn't hear me. Very unprofessional. I tried to untie her hands; the ropes were tight and the knots massive. It was difficult with my wrists bound behind me. When I tired Jenny would work on mine.

I was terrified that they were going to kill us. That they were going to take us deep into the woods and dump our lifeless bodies someplace where nobody would ever find them. The longer the ride lasted the greater this fear became.

It's strange but I couldn't stop thinking about my dad. If something happened to me I know he'd just fall apart. First my mom, now me—it would be too much. He never talked about my mother and I always understood why. It was too painful for him. In two months

Jenny has told me more about her than my dad has in my entire life.

I tried to keep focused on untying Jenny's wrists, to push the negative thoughts out of my head. I tried to think of anything my dad taught me that might come in handy but it was difficult to concentrate with the game blasting and the smothering fear that wouldn't go away.

Jenny's long fingers and sharp fingernails seem to be having an effect on my knotted rope. It definitely feels looser. It's a start. Dams don't just break all at once; they start with a little leak. This is my leak. If the duct tape wasn't so tight across my mouth I might even smile.

When the van finally stops, the Yankees are winning four to two.

The men sit for a while and wait for the inning to end before opening the sliding door and pulling us outside. They don't say anything, just "Walk," before pushing us in one direction. It feels like we're on an old parking lot, full of holes and broken curbs; it's difficult to hike across with this duct tape on my eyes. Dawg laughs whenever I trip.

There's a loud grinding, crunching noise off in the distance; it sounds familiar, like what I used to hear in the background when my dad called. Maybe it's nothing to get excited about, just a similar sound, but maybe it means something.

It seems like we walk forever but it's hard to tell; when you can't see where you're going even the shortest distance feels too far.

I don't dare work on the ropes. I'm worried one of the guys will notice. Eventually we're led through a door.

Inside, it smells old and musty. There's a cold, stale dampness to the air. Each step we take and each door that's opened or closed echoes loudly, leaving me to believe that we're in a large abandoned factory.

Eventually we're led into a room and forced into hard wooden chairs. Dawg roughly ties me to mine and I can hear Dude doing the same to Jenny.

They leave the duct tape on our mouths and eyes. Not being able to talk or see is beginning to take its toll. It makes me feel powerless; it heightens my fear. It's like I'm drowning.

After a while Dude snorts, "Okay, good enough, turn on the game already."

The game comes pumping into the room, the sound echoes around me. There's something oddly comforting about it. Even though everything here is crazy, out there something is stable and moving along, following a strict set of rules and regulations. If there's structure somewhere, this chaos can't last forever.

The Mets manage to scratch out another run but a new Yankee pitcher comes into the game and starts striking out one Met batter after another. I keep working on the ropes; they're definitely getting looser. Dawg and Dude cheer loudly after each strikeout.

It doesn't look good for the Mets. It's the bottom of the ninth and the Yankee pitcher strikes out the first batter with three pitches. I can't believe this dumb game is pushing its way into my head. Dawg walks over to us and practically shouts, "You guys are Met fans, aren't you? I saw the hat in your kitchen."

I nod my head, I don't know why, and apparently Jenny did the same because a moment later the tape is violently ripped off our eyes and mouths. It feels like half my eyebrows were removed with the tape.

Dawg has a huge grin below his surprisingly large swollen nose. He points at us and barks, "Your loser team is going down. Sit here and watch the Yankees win another World Series. Ain't that right, Dude?"

"Got that right!" The two of them laugh like it's the most hilarious thing anyone has ever said before. Is there something wrong with these guys?

There's a television on a desk across the room. Dawg runs over and flops onto an old couch set up in front of it. He turns and grins. "Your team's going bye-bye."

Dude is standing over by a large window. It's open and there are bags of sand stacked up in front of it. He's dividing his time between scanning the yard outside with his rifle and looking at the game.

Something about the way Dawg moved across the room seems familiar to me. What is it? The waitress's smile and her little wink suddenly flash into my head, and I remember how the large man ran from the blue car right before the explosion.

He ran exactly like Dawg, and like the waitress's wink, it's something I'll never forget.

The words come out of my mouth before I even have time to think about them. "Hey, you did it! You were the one who blew up that café!"

He looks over the top of the couch. "Quiet, kid, or I'm taping your mouth shut again!"

Jenny mutters, "Cody, try to control yourself."

I ignore her and shout, "You killed all those people! What's wrong with you?"

"I'm warning you! Shut up or you're getting taped."

The words keep flowing, it's like I have no control over them. "But they didn't do anything! Twelve people died that day. You killed twelve people! Why? What's wrong with you?"

He turns around and throws a soda can at me. I move my head and it sails past my shoulder. "Didn't I tell you to shut up? It should have been fourteen! I don't know how you and your dad walked away from that one."

"But why?"

Dawg quickly gets up from the couch and marches across the room. He grabs the roll of duct tape and rips off a piece and slaps it across my mouth and then slaps one over Jenny's mouth, too.

He glares at me. "Why? Because it was payback time. You guys cost my boss a lot of money. He had a good thing going down in South America until your dad came along and broke it all up."

Dude yells from the window, "Knock it off! Don't tell them anything. What's wrong with you? Boss told us to hold them, he didn't say anything about arguing with them."

He looks at me. "Kid, be quiet, okay? My boss just wants to meet with your dad. When he does you'll be free to leave."

Yeah, like I believe that. I examine the room, looking for potential weapons and different avenues of escape. There are so many possibilities. All the doors are open and there's even a knife on one of the desks. Once again I question the professionalism of our captors. They seem to be doing everything wrong.

I glance over at Jenny. We make eye contact. I can tell she's scared but I can also tell she loves and cares for me. I realize I love her, too. There's so much I want to tell her. I hope we get the chance.

I'm determined to get these ropes off my wrists. I'm not just going to sit here and hope for the best. I work my finger through a small opening and pull. I can feel the rope suddenly loosen further. I pull my wrist upward and it slips through to freedom. I start to untie the rest of the ropes.

I'm careful. I work slowly. I don't want anyone to notice what I'm doing.

Jenny looks at me, and realizing I've untied my ropes, she gives me a little nod of approval then flicks her head toward the back of the room. I know what she's trying to say. She wants me to leave her and run if I get a chance.

I shake my head no and I mean it. I'm not leaving without her.

"Yeah!" Dawg starts clapping his hands. He looks over at us. I keep my hands behind my back. "One more strike and this game is over!"

I stare at the screen; I can't help myself. The pitch comes inside, the batter tries to get out of the way but it bounces off his thigh. He runs down to first base.

Dawg is up on his feet. "Oh, man! Dude, did you see that? He had him! He didn't even try to get out of the way. This game should be over!"

It seems like the next batter is up forever. He keeps fouling off one pitch after another. It's become more than just a baseball game to me. The tension is unbearable. Dude leaves his post by the window and joins Dawg in front of the screen.

I notice that his gun is still next to the window. This is it, the opening I've been waiting for. If I can get the rest of the ropes off my legs fast enough there's a really good chance I could get to that gun before he does.

The noise level of the game suddenly increases; there's a surge of excitement and urgency. I look at the screen and see the camera tracking a baseball sailing through the night sky. The announcer is shouting, "Long fly ball . . . deep to center field . . . this one's going to be close . . . Damon's at the wall . . . he jumps . . . did he get it . . . no . . . it's a . . . home run. Mets win! Mets win!"

Dawg kicks over a chair and Dude starts to curse loudly.

Thump.

Andy jumps in through the window, rushes across the room, and places a gun against Dawg's head. He yells, "Nobody move!"

Dude makes a move toward the rifle and Andy quickly fires a shot into the television. The sound is deafening. It's like an explosion, the sound echoing all around the large empty building. "Next one goes into your head."

Dude stops moving and raises his hands.

I get the final rope off my legs and rush across the room and grab the rifle. I point it at Dude.

Andy looks at me. "You know how to use that thing?"

"An AK-47? Come on, it's the simplest weapon in the world. I've read that you can take them apart and put them back together again blindfolded."

"No need to try that now, just cover me." He looks around the room. "Is there anyone else?"

I'm surprised how heavy the gun feels in my hands. I know it doesn't weigh much but it has its own kind of dense weight. My hands start shaking. This thing could kill everyone in the room with just a twitch of my finger. I can feel its deadly power; it feels alive, angry, and vicious. It's making me nervous.

"Cody!"

"Huh?"

Andy seems annoyed. "I said is there anyone else here?"

I glance around. "Not that I know of."

He points at Jenny. "Get her out of those ropes."

I grab the knife off the desk, run over and quickly cut away her ropes. She pulls the tape away from her mouth, stands up and throws her arms around me. "Are you okay, hon?"

"I'm good." I kiss the side of her head. "I love you, Aunt Jenny."

She's smiling and crying at the same time. "I love you too. I was so worried something would happen to you."

Andy yells, "Cody, bring me the rope!"

I run to his side with the rope and tape. He gives Jenny his gun. "You know how to use this?"

"Like a camera, point and shoot?"

He nods. "Yeah, that will work. I'm going to tie up our two friends while you and Cody keep them honest with your guns. But first give me that knife."

I hand him the knife and he quickly slices the clothes off the two men. He makes it look easier than peeling an orange. Dawg and Dude are soon left standing in their underwear, shivering from both fear and the cold, damp air. There's no need to worry about concealed weapons now.

Andy takes the ropes and moves with the speed of a rodeo

cowboy binding a couple calves. A moment later they're tied to chairs; these guys aren't going anywhere.

When the men are finally secured, Andy seems to relax a little. It's strange how I didn't notice how nervous he was until now. He lets out a long breath of air. "Who are these guys?"

"They work . . . " My voice cracks. I guess I'm nervous, too. I push on, "They work for that arms dealer." I point at Dawg and can hear the anger rising in my voice. "Guess what? He's the one who blew up the café. He killed all those people."

Andy snatches the pistol away from Jenny, stomps over to Dawg, and jams the gun against his head. For a second I think he's going to pull the trigger. Instead he starts talking in a calm, lifeless voice that is somehow incredibly terrifying. "I've had it with worthless garbage like you killing innocent bystanders, so here's my question: Is there anyone else in this building I should know about? You only get one chance to answer."

Dawg's eyes open wide with sudden terror. He blubbers, "No . . . just me and Dude. Really. We were told to hold the woman and boy until we heard from the boss."

Andy pushes his head with the gun and asks, "How was he going to contact you?"

"Cell phone . . . he was going to call our cell phone."

Andy points the gun at Dude. "That true? Nobody else is here? Nobody's coming?"

Dude shakes his head so hard it looks like it might fall off.

Then he says, "Yeah, it's true. Don't kill us, please."

Andy turns and glares at me, and for a moment I don't recognize him. He seems possessed, there's a fierce, wild look in his eyes, he looks more animal than man. There's not a doubt in my mind that I'm looking at a brutal warrior who has killed many people in the service of his country. I'd never seen this side of him before. I'm shocked, it's like stepping on a garden hose and discovering it's a snake.

I take a few steps backward and his face suddenly changes. I think he can see the fear in my eyes. I watch him take a deep breath and slowly let it out. He closes his eyes and his face softens, becomes calmer, less threatening. When he opens his eyes again they belong to the Andy I know.

He shakes his head and looks at Dude and Dawg. "We're spending too much time here. Let's lock them up someplace and get out of here. No sense waiting around for trouble. I'll make some calls when we're safe."

We tape their eyes and mouths before adding more rope. The three of us quickly push them across the floor, lock them in a closet, and move a heavy desk in front of it.

Jenny's got a huge smile on her face as she pats the dust and dirt off her shirt and pants. "That felt really good. I know it shouldn't have, but tying those guys up after what they did to us was very therapeutic."

I start to laugh. "Yeah, I know what you mean. Andy did

that . . ." He's gone. I look around the room and he's nowhere in sight, it's like he just vanished.

"What happened to Andy?"

Jenny glances around the room. "I don't know. He was just here a second ago."

I yell, "Andy!"

We quickly search the room before checking the hall. I jump because he's standing just a few feet beyond the door. I notice that his gun is on the floor in front of him. "Hey, what are you doing? We were beginning to wonder if you fell in a hole or something."

He doesn't smile. There's panic in his eyes, then I notice a dark, masked figure standing in the shadows behind him with the barrel of a gun placed in the center of his back.

The man in black hisses from the darkness, "Slowly place your hand behind your head."

There's something about his voice.

Andy does as he's told.

"Now kick the gun over to the boy and get on your knees."

I know that voice.

The Glock slides across the floor and I pick it up. What's going on? As Andy moves to his knees, I strain to get a good look at the man in black, the bulletproof vest under his jacket making him seem larger, the black ski mask, the Swiss Army watch peeking out from below his sleeve.

I can't believe that he's really here. I swallow hard. "Dad, is that you?"

He steps into the light and slowly pulls the ski mask off. There's the familiar beard, the piercing blue eyes, the long scar on his cheek. "Yes, son, it's me."

I want to run and throw my arms around him and tell him I've missed him, but there's also this part of me that wants to hit him, scream and shout, and to tell him how much I hate all this. I'm torn between this love and hate and I wind up not doing anything. I just stand here, lost somewhere in the past and confused by the present.

"Dad, Andy's my friend. He's been helping me. You don't have to point your gun at him."

He looks at me. "There's something not quite right here. Remember how I told you that you've got to trust your gut? My gut tells me he's working for someone."

I glance over at Jenny. She's terrified. I guess I never realized how scary my dad could be.

"Dad, stop pointing the gun at Andy."

"Son, think about it. Use your head—why didn't he call the police? What do you really know about this man?"

I snort. "I know he just saved me! Where were you?"

"I was always by your side, always watching. I wouldn't have let anything happen. I knew they'd come after you to get to me. This was the only logical way to eliminate our problem."

It sinks in. I shout, "You mean you used me as *bait*? I don't believe it! How could you do that to me?"

"You weren't bait. Bait is something you sacrifice. We're a team. We work together. You were never in any danger."

Jenny snaps, "Robert, what are you talking about? Men with guns kidnapped us! Cody was beat up!"

"He was perfectly safe. I would never let anything happen to him."

Andy mutters, "Yeah right. That's why he was almost blown to bits."

My dad pushes him with the gun. "How do you know about that? See, Cody, this man knows more than he should."

"It's because I told him what was going on."

He looks stunned. "Why would you do that? You know you're not supposed to tell anyone what we do. It's our number-one rule."

My voice strains, "Because I needed help."

Something dawns on me and it's like my head explodes. "I don't believe it!" I point at him. "That was you in the woods! Wasn't it?"

My dad nods.

I throw up my arms. "How was I supposed to know that? Guns, wireless cameras—I didn't know what I was up against! I needed help. I trusted *my* gut. I trusted Andy. Why didn't you trust me with the truth?"

"Son, try to understand. It was important that we didn't tip our hand. We had to make everything look like you just moved here and you were trying to start a new life. I was close, really close, to ending all this. One more day and I would have caught everyone responsible and we could have been on our way. They just moved a little quicker than I thought they would."

I practically shout, "But you used me as bait! You could have at least told me what the plan was."

Anger slips into his voice. "Don't you take that tone with me. I worked out a plan, the best plan for the situation. It was imperative that you behaved naturally. You wouldn't have acted natural had you known the plan."

My dad looks down at Andy and pokes him again with the gun. "But I've got a big question for your one-armed friend here. Anyone else would have called the police, especially when these two were kidnapped. Why didn't you?"

"I used to work for military intelligence."

"So?"

"So, a few days ago I made a phone call to an old friend who's about as connected as you can be. It didn't take long before someone came knocking on my door. He told me to observe, report, and above all not to involve the local police."

Andy looks at me. "Cody, I was wrong. Only a few people know this, but your dad's still with the Agency. He has a lot of freedom but he's still with them. The stories about the New Order aren't true. That's his cover; it's allowed him to do some truly great things. He's not some renegade running around the world with his own agenda, he's one of our top agents. I know I should have told you before but I didn't get the chance."

My dad removes the gun from Andy's back. "If you were able to find that out maybe I *do* have something to worry about. I'm just trying to do what's right. It's all about keeping our country safe."

Jenny reaches down and helps Andy to his feet. She glares at my dad. "Don't you think it's time you made sure Cody's safe, too? This is crazy."

"He is safe. Listen, you can be hit by a car walking across the street. There are no guarantees in life; you just do what you have to do. If I didn't think he was safe, I'd let him stay with you, but trust me, he's safe."

Andy brushes off the knees of his pants before turning to my dad. "Talking about being safe, we've been here way too long. Maybe we could have this conversation someplace else? I'd like to get out of here. *My* gut tells me to move on."

"Fair enough."

"Can I give him his gun back?" My dad nods and I hand it over.

Dad gives me his first real smile of the night. He holds out his arms. "Before we go, aren't you forgetting something?"

I move toward his outstretched arms but at the last minute I'm overcome with rage. I start beating on his chest. The vest feels hard under my fists. "I hate you. Why did you use me like that?" He puts his arms around me and holds me tight.

I mutter, "Why didn't you trust me? I love you, but this is all wrong. I can't believe you did this to me."

He rubs my back and whispers into my ear. "Everything will be different now. I promise."

I push myself away from him. "Dad, was this really all about the arms dealer? The café? All those dead people? That's what this was all about? I thought you said they were nobody."

He shakes his head. "We've gone against some of the most powerful people in the world, and the one that comes after me was a small-time arms dealer out of New York. Just goes to show you: never underestimate a determined underdog."

I can hear the frustration in my voice. "That's it? Don't underestimate an underdog? How about don't underestimate anyone! All those people are dead."

My dad just stands there. For once he seems to be at a loss for words. Finally he says, "You're right. I've realized we have to be more careful. From now on we'll be a complete team, total trust, covering every track. Truth is, I need you."

He reaches out and pulls me close again. I hold him tight. Even with the bulky vest wrapped around his chest he feels familiar and safe; his smell brings back pleasant memories. I don't ever want to let go but there's also this huge part of me that wants to push him away.

Andy looks down the hall toward the door. "Hey, guys, you can talk all this through later. I think it's time to get going."

We follow Andy down the long hall and out a glass door leading to a parking lot. The air is crisp and clean, and the sky is full of stars. It feels good to finally be outside, to begin to relax, to be free, to be alive.

My dad looks over his shoulder. "Did I hear that you tried to fight one of those big guys?"

"Well, let's just say I—"

About thirty feet ahead of us a shadow darts out from behind a building and raises something toward my dad.

I try to push him out of the way. He stumbles to the right. Everything seems to slow down.

There's a noise.

Something kicks me hard in the chest.

It shoves me backward.

Picking me off my feet.

I crash through a plate-glass window.

I slam down on the hard tile floor.

Small pieces of glass shower down around me. I'm looking up at the ceiling. *What happened? Did someone push me? I feel so strange.*

My arms are spread out wide; my legs are bent and twisted. There are mounds of little glittering, perfect squares of glass covering my body and the floor. They're beautiful, like diamonds. I guess I'm rich.

Outside something's popping.

Pop.

Pop.

Pop.

Is someone playing with Bubble Wrap? That's a funny idea. I try to laugh. It sounds like an old, broken rattle.

Jenny's suddenly leaning over me; her eyes are wide with panic. She's shouting, "Cody! Oh, my God! Cody!"

The words come out of my mouth slowly. "What . . . happened?"

She shrieks, "Honey, you were shot. Oh, god. Hold on, okay . . . you're going to be okay."

Shot? I was shot? Is that what she said? I turn my head to the side, the glass crunches as I move. There's blood on the tiles. Lots of blood, it can't all be mine.

My dad and Andy are leaning over me now. My dad looks as frantic as Jenny. They look so scared. Everyone's moving strangely, like a movie that keeps stopping and starting over and over.

"Hang in there, son. We got the guy. You just stay strong."

My dad grabs my feet; Andy has one of my wrists and Jenny has the other. They lift me up and start running. *Where are we going?* It feels like I'm flying on a magic carpet, sailing across the parking lot.

Andy's yelling, "No more! Hasn't there been enough of this? No more!"

Jenny's crying; I want to tell her everything's going to be okay but the words don't come out. Maybe if I think them really hard she'll hear me.

I'm lying in the backseat of Annie's car. The top's down and I'm surrounded by the night. *How did I get here?* Jenny's on top of me, her knees on either side of my chest, she's pressing something against where I got shot. It doesn't hurt, nothing hurts.

Andy's in the front yelling, "Keep pressure on it! Push as hard as you can!"

My dad's driving. We're going so fast, maybe too fast. The huge engine roars through the night. The tires screech around corners. He's constantly honking the horn and shouting, "Get out of the way!"

Jenny's crying and yelling, "Stay with me, Cody! Stay with me!" She's covered in blood.

Above her I can see the stars. They're so beautiful, thousands—no, maybe millions of stars filling every inch of the sky.

I look closely. I move toward them. Together they look like snow. I find myself blending into them. It's cold and I like it.

I'm skiing with my dad again back in the French Alps, tackling that incredibly steep trail called Dead Man's Drop.

I'm planting my pole, swinging my body, and hopping. Planting my pole, swinging my body, and hopping. I'm gaining on my dad, sinking deeper into the snow. It feels like I'm riding a white wave. I start to laugh. The cold air feels great against my face. I love the rush, the excitement, the danger.

Dad glances back at me, grins, and shouts, "Now this is living!"

I zoom past him with a large smile stretched across my face. I yell, "Out of my way, old man!"

"Cody?"

"Cody!"

I focus on the voice. There's a man looking down at me. He's wearing a New York Mets baseball cap. He's shining a light in my eyes.

"Cody, can you hear me? Say something."

I go to say yes but it comes out as a moan instead. He seems to understand me anyway.

"Good. . . . Cody, you've been shot, do you understand?"

I moan my yes.

"Good. You're in the emergency room. I'm a doctor. You're going to be okay."

He's still hovering over me, looking down; I notice the florescent lights behind him, the white walls and curtains. I focus on his cap.

I say, "World . . . Champs."

"What's that?" He leans in close and puts his ear right against my mouth.

I repeat, but this time a little more forceful, "World Champs."

He stands up, smiles, and touches the cap. "That's right, buddy. World Champs. We finally beat the Yankees."

AWAKE

During the day everything's brighter, the light comes with its own hope, and the warm comfort that there are better days ahead. There's activity, noise, and people constantly visiting. Laughter can be heard. Jenny sits by my side. Renee sometimes stays for hours. The pain doesn't seem that bad.

The nights are different. A quiet settles around the hospital. If I'm awake in these dark, late night hours, overwhelmed by pain and loneliness, I'll think about my past and wonder about the future. It's then that I feel marooned. I'm the forgotten astronaut left stranded on some strange, distant planet.

I snap my eyes open, after clawing my way out of another bad dream: the blood, the shattered plate-glass window, Jenny screaming. I glance at the digital clock. 2:37. I moan and feel the dull, aching pain in my chest and shoulder flare back into existence. It's going to be a long night. I better call the nurse for something to help me sleep.

There's a button that I've got to push. It's around here somewhere. I grope for it in the darkness. I glance toward the corner of the room and freeze. Someone's sitting in a chair looking at me. I can see the dark outline of his body. I make a quick inventory of my surroundings for potential weapons, not that it matters—I doubt I'd be able to fight right now.

"Cody, you awake?"

"Dad? Is that you?"

"Yes . . . here, let me turn on a light."

His dark shadow moves across the room to the nightstand and a moment later the small lamp blazes to life with its low-wattage bulb.

The lamp isn't very bright but I still blink as my eyes adjust to the light. "What are you doing here? You nearly gave me a heart attack."

He quietly pulls the curtain closed around us before moving a chair close to my bed. "This is the safest time for me to visit. Sorry I wasn't here before, I couldn't take the chance."

"I understand."

My dad leans forward. "I've read all of your files, and it looks like you're going to be fine. It's going to take you a couple months of rehabilitation but they expect a one-hundred-percent recovery."

I try to smile but I can't. Did he say "months"?

"What about the arms dealer? Did you take care of him?"

My dad grins. "Everything's been taken care of. We shut him down completely. Good thing, too. There was more to him than we thought. He was putting a lot of weapons into the hands of people who should never have them."

I nod my head and the two of us sit together in the dark silence. It shouldn't be this hard to talk to my dad. These long moments of silence never bothered me before I started living with Jenny.

He's leaning over my bed. His wide shoulders and muscles are barely contained under his jacket. He looks so strong, tough, and brave.

"Dad?"

"Yes, son."

"I didn't do too well back there. I was so scared." I stare up at the ceiling remembering how I felt that night. "I thought for sure that they were going to kill us. I wasn't brave at all. I wanted to be like you, but I couldn't do it. I'm sorry."

He smiles and shakes his head. "Hey, you did fine. Don't go looking at me. I'm not that brave. When you were shot—I don't think I've ever been more scared in my life."

"No, Dad. You're the bravest man I've ever known."

He doesn't say anything for a long time. When he starts to talk his voice is eerily calm. "Listen, what I should have done, if

I was brave enough . . . What I should have done is let your aunt Jenny raise you. That way you would have had a proper childhood. You should have friends, different teachers, and a house to call a home." He smiles. "At the very least, you shouldn't have to change your name every other week."

I look at my dad and I want to tell him that "No, my childhood was just fine, I wouldn't want to change a thing," but I can't get myself to say the words. What does that mean? I don't think it's too hard to figure out.

He's the only permanent thing in my life, but I want more. I'm tired of traveling the world. I'm tired of never having friends. I'm just tired.

I reach out and grab his large hand. "Maybe I should stay with Aunt Jenny until I'm better. I could try to finish the school year, too."

My dad's hand grips mine harder. I glance over at him and he has his head bowed, studying our hands. He's quiet for a long time. Finally he looks up and says, "High school starts next year. I loved high school. Maybe you should . . . you know . . . give it a try." He tries to smile but there's no life behind it. "I can visit, and if you ever need me, I'll be on the next plane."

I don't know what to say. I want to say yes but I don't want to hurt his feelings.

He gives my hand a squeeze. "Tell you what. We'll just play it month by month for now. You just focus on getting better. Okay?"

"Okay . . . and Dad?"

"Yes, son?"

"I love you."

He reaches down, holds me tight, and whispers in a voice that sounds close to tears, "I love you too, Cody. Take good care of your aunt Jenny."

don't want to ride in a wheelchair."

Jenny throws up her arms. "Cody, we've been over this. It's just policy. This is the procedure for being discharged. You want to get out of here, right?"

I look at Jenny and the nurse. The nurse looks like she's slowly losing her patience.

"Of course I want to get out of here. I just don't want anyone to see me in a wheelchair."

The nurse pushes the chair over to me. She forcefully says, "Just get in. I'll have you out of here in two minutes."

Something about the look on her face convinces me to quickly get into the chair. I don't believe she's a woman you say no to.

When we're riding down the elevator, the nurse says, "You're very fortunate to survive such a terrible hunting accident. I think you're destined for special things in this life."

I don't know what to say but Jenny says, "I think you're right."

I'm amazed at how quickly we're out of the hospital and into

Jenny's Jeep. When they tell you it's time to go, you're gone.

It was raining for the last three days but today it's a clear warm day. I roll down the window. The fresh air feels good against my face. The radio sounds good; they're playing something I heard in the hospital.

"Hey, can you turn up this song?"

Jenny gives me a smile as she turns up the volume. "I like this too, it's fun."

We slowly drive through the now familiar town. It's nice to be out of the hospital. I forgot how great it is just to drive around. There's a strange sense of freedom to it all. It's enough to make you want to do something really stupid, like sing along to the radio, but I don't.

We pull into Jenny's street. She reaches over and pats me on my knee. "Hey, almost home."

Home? It does feel like I'm going home. All of the traveling I've done, all of the special places I've seen, none of them has impressed me as much as that little backyard cottage in the Connecticut woods.

"Aunt Jenny?"

"Yeah, hon?"

I search for the words. "I just want to say . . . that I, um, well . . . you know."

She reaches out and squeezes my shoulder. "I know. I love you, too."

We pull into our driveway. I notice a huge banner stretched across the front of the yellow house. It's the same one they put out for Andy. It says WELCOME HOME.

Jenny slowly drives down the driveway. There's a crowd of people by the garage. It takes me a second to realize they're all waiting for me.

When we get to the garage everyone starts cheering. I look around. There's Albert and his mother with huge smiles. Pogo, Frank, and the rest of the karate club kids are there too.

Troy Sampson's the only guy still wearing a tie. Amber and Nicki are standing by his side.

Renee's the first one to the door and she has it open before the Jeep's even to a full stop. Seeing her face is like turning on a light in a dark room.

Cell Phone Girl is over to the side smiling at me; she has her phone pressed against her ear.

When I get out of the Jeep, my arm still in a sling, I nod to Andy, who has one of the largest smiles in the crowd.

OPENING DAY

"Ladies and gentleman, will you please rise for the playing of our national anthem."

I stand and glance down the aisle. Frank, Pogo, and Albert are joking about something. Annie has her arm draped across Andy's back, and Jenny and Renee are quietly talking. Who knows what they're plotting.

When the music starts everyone grows serious and turns their attention to the flag flying out in centerfield.

I watch the flag, suddenly overcome with emotion. I keep my eyes focused on it, willing myself not to cry; that would be so embarrassing.

I remember waking up in that hospital bed, Jenny by my side; she was crying. There were all these wires and tubes snaking out of my body, feeding into machines that beeped and hummed. I didn't know where I was at first and I jumped, full of panic and alarm.

Jenny reached out and calmed me down. She sat by my side all day long and every day after that.

Something about all those wires and tubes . . . I began to think of them as a fence between my old life with my dad and my new life with Jenny. A wall that would remain long after the doctors removed them.

In the early days of my recovery, Jenny made me a promise that she'd get us tickets for next season's opening day. She said I'd walk into that stadium feeling one hundred percent again. I remember doubting her that day. I was convinced I'd never feel better, but it turned out she was right.

The last six months have been some of the best of my life. I have Aunt Jenny, Renee, and lots of friends. I even managed to hang a few things on my bedroom wall: a nice painting Renee made for me while I was in the hospital and a couple of baseball posters.

The crowd cheers, the anthem's over. Andy reaches over and gives me a light punch on the arm.

"And now taking the field, it's your World Champion New York Mets!"

The players run onto the field, scattering in different directions, stopping at their positions. First base first, left field last. I listen to everyone cheering around me, cheering louder than I've ever heard before. I clap my hands together as hard as I possibly can and cheer right along with them.

I love the sound of the crowd and being a part of it.

I love baseball.

"DO I HAVE FAMILY IN THE IMAGINE NATION?" JACK ASKED. "ARE THEY SUPERHEROES?"

"YOU'RE A MYSTERY, JACK. BUT THAT'S ALL ABOUT TO CHANGE."

DON'T MISS THE THRILLING ADVENTURE of Jack Blank, who could be either the savior of the Imagine Nation and the world beyond, or the biggest threat they've ever faced. And even Jack himself doesn't know which it will be. . . .

From Aladdin

KIDS.SimonandSchuster.com

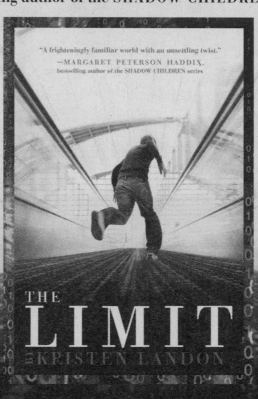